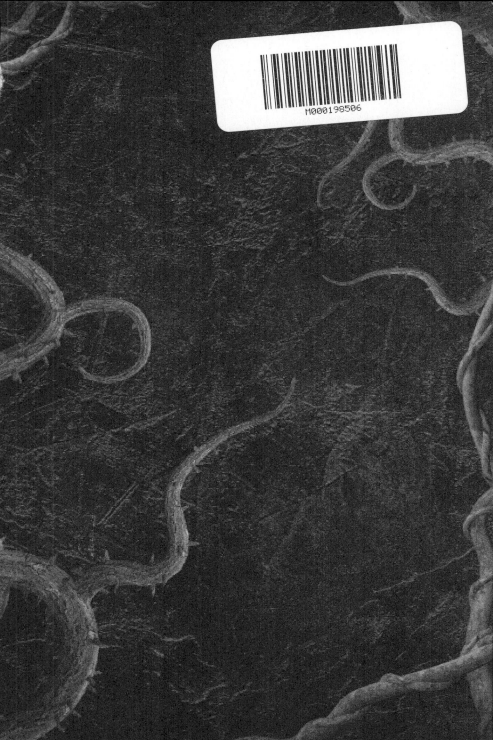

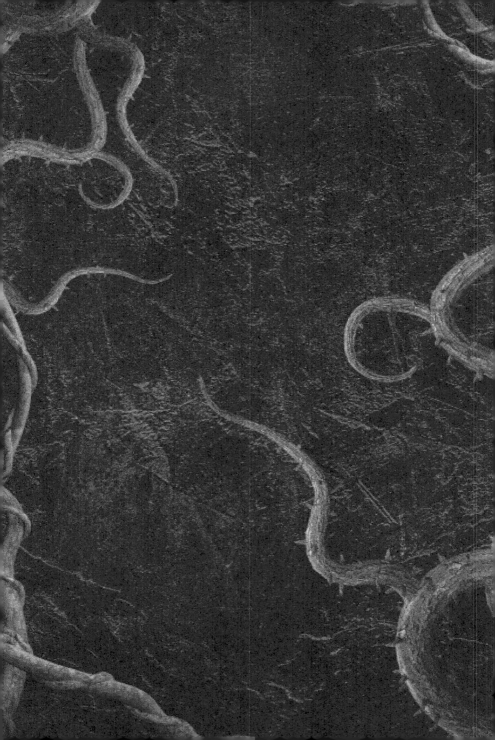

# Also by Danielle Annett

# Before You Begin

This book is recommended for mature readers 17+
Cruel Wolves & Devious Deceptions was originally published as a
contemporary romance novel under my romance pen name.

When word spread that I branched out into writing contemporary
romance, my fantasy readers requested I give them a paranormal
version of my contemporary book and I was happy to oblige.

Cruel Wolves & Devious Deceptions is 15,000 words longer than
the contemporary version and took twice as long to complete as the
original. I may have shot myself in the foot when I agreed to do this
but regardless, I hope you enjoy Meiying & Desmond's story.

Please note, unlike previous books in the series, this story is not a
standalone novel. Cruel Wolves & Devious Deceptions is part
one of a two part duet and will conclude in
Cruel Promises & Twisted Temptations.

# Chaper One

## Meiying

There's this sense of foreboding thrumming through me as I look up at the impeccably manicured lawns and twin pillars that decorate where I'll be living this next school year. All one hundred and eighty days of it, plus winter and spring breaks. I'm going to hate every minute of it.

The local council decided that since Hellbound High was such a success, why not open the doors to interspecies education and full integration within the local colleges too. The first few years were a little rocky, but now supposedly it's been smooth sailing enough so that it's become a requirement for all people residing within city limits to attend between the ages of eighteen and twenty-two.

A minimum four-year enrollment is required to secure peace and intermixing between the factions. And that's great and all. I'm all for mixing. One of my best friends is a hydrokinetic after all, and I know the opportunity this presents. Before Hellbound U opened up, my education would have been limited to Pack instructors once I graduated high school. But I'm a tiger which means I like my space. I'm a solitary creature. And living in -campus housing, away from my clan, my *pack*, is a nightmare come true.

*I shu••er.*

To make matters worse, Mom decided I needed to join the Kappa Eagle house, because a traditional dorm wasn't bad enough. Kappa Eagle is a wannabe paranormal sorority, and she thinks it'll be a positive experience for me. Something to do with making friends and stepping out of my comfort zone.

I call bullshit.

Mom wants to leave the Pack. She was invited to the South Atlantic Pack Summit and thinks she met her mate while she was there, you know, for the whole three days she had to get to know the guy.

I huff out a breath. I shouldn't be such a pessimist. If she met her one true mate, that's great. I want Mom to be happy. She and Dad obviously didn't work out, not that we didn't all see that coming, but Mom falls in love hard and fast. Her relationships never last more than a few months and the only reason she wants to leave is because she's already made her way through everyone here in Clan Cat and according to her, she'd never stoop to looking for someone outside of her Clan again nor will she mate with *another white man who •oesn't appreciate her culture*. I guess Zheng's Dad being human and mine being the man *who can't appreciate her culture* and all left a lasting impression. Now she's determined to mate with a tiger, preferably one of Asian descent, and live happily ever after.

She suggested I go with her. There aren't any other tigers in our Clan around my age, but I'm not looking for my forever mate at the ripe age of seventeen, and I'm in no hurry to leave my brother or friends behind. Also, because it's worth mentioning, I don't care what kind of animal my mate shifts into or what ethnicity he is. If it's love, it's love. None of the rest matters, so she can take her elitist bullshit and keep it to herself. I don't need that noise in my life.

Which brings me to Kappa Eagle.

Paranormal sorority hell. And no, I don't have any firsthand experience with sororities, and yes, I'm absolutely judging them based on what I've seen on television, but let's be real, if you knew anything about me, you'd agree that me and the perfect plastics I see walking in and out of the houses on sorority row aren't a match made in heaven. No one here is going to understand what it's like to be a shifter. As far as I know, I'm the only Pack member moving in. What if they hate me? Or end up being afraid of me? Which isn't unheard of. Things might be better since the Awakening, when paranormals came out and announced to the humans that we were here. But there are always those pockets of people who think paranormals, and shifters in particular, should be caged. That we're wild savages at risk of going rogue at any moment.

I chew on my bottom lip and do my best to force away my anxiety. Hellbound High was fine. Hellbound U will be fine too.

When I applied for Hellbound High's running start program—a program that allows me to attend college courses and earn both college credits and the final credits I'll need for my high school diploma, I thought, *this is exactly what I nee•.* An escape from the stupid drama that is high school life where I never really fit in. It's hard to relate to the people at school when all they can talk about is how Suzie made out with Jason behind Ruby's back and other stupid nonsense, like who is asking who to senior prom. Public high school isn't required for all factions now that the university is open, and once Zheng and the others graduated, I was virtually on my own.

Meanwhile, my best friends have all graduated and are planning their mating ceremonies and being moms and doing real-life things that matter. It makes it hard to relate to high-school life. Hearing the gossip and then seeing all the back-stabby antics, it's not what I'm interested in. And don't even get me started on the boys.

They're so incredibly stupid in high school. The catcalling and fuck-boy flirting. Urgh. You'd think they'd find a better pickup line than, "You must be an angel, because you look like you just fell from heaven."

Barf.

*No asshole. I'm a tiger an• here, let me show you my teeth an• claws.*

The guys I go to school with have zero game. Not that I'd be interested in anyone at Hellbound High anyway. I almost wish I was. It'd make seeing a certain broody wolf on the regular a hell of a lot easier, and both of us attending the same college isn't going to help.

Hellbound University is his turf, and here he reigns supreme, not that I'm surprised. Desmond Pierce and his Clan mates Rafael and Jordy ran the halls of Hellbound High as the school's shifter gods, so of course their reputations would follow them to college as they continue to dominate even more now with the introduction of *Infernum.* The

University's solution to athletics between factions which means "hell" in Latin. And trust me, it's an accurate name for that game.

Anyone can play, and as far as rules go, there are few. It's brutal and bloody and one of the few chances people have to really let themselves loose and see what they're capable of. Even vamps play, since all games take place after sundown. It's insane and super intense.

Not that I'd ever admit to watching Desmond and the others play. It'd go to their heads, and I'm not one for stoking wolf egos.

I used to hate those three for what they put my brother through, but now we're all friends. Hell, more like family, if I'm honest. But I don't need people realizing we know each other, especially with the unwanted attention that will bring.

"Ready to braid hair and paint your nails bubblegum pink?" my brother—Zheng—asks from the front seat.

I roll my eyes and flip him the bird. "Ha. Ha. You're so funny."

He turns to glance at me, pushing his jet black hair from his face to give me a wink. "Don't worry, sis. They'll leave you alone once they realize what a prickly personality you have."

I lunge forward on a growl, but he swings open the passenger side door, stepping out just in time to avoid my swipe.

"Meiying!" my mother admonishes me.

"What? He started it," I tell her as I unbuckle to follow him. Despite the early hour, the house is already buzzing with activity— what looks to be a party in full swing. Girls in all manner of summer wear are flitting about, socializing, drinking whatever is in those red Solo cups—and let's be honest, it's not water—and carrying boxes, doing exactly what I'm here to do. Move in.

I wrinkle my nose and glance at my mom as she slings her oversized purse over her shoulder and moves to join Zheng and me on the sidewalk. "Not too late to change your mind," Zheng mutters under his breath. "You know you wanna."

I elbow him in the ribs. "Are we telling jokes now?"

When mom concocted this grand idea of me joining a sorority, Zheng, being the protective big brother he is, was nice enough to offer me the spare room at his place. An offer I was quick to decline.

Under normal circumstances, I'd consider it. We were never very close growing up given the four-year age gap between us, but Zheng has always looked out for me. Most brothers would balk at the idea of living with their baby sister after they moved out, but Zheng genuinely wouldn't mind. He's pretty chill about stuff like that.

The problem isn't living with my brother. It's living with my brother's very hot, very broody, drives-me-insane, asshole of a wolf roommate—Desmond Pierce. On the best of days, we tolerate one another. On the worst, well, things can be openly hostile.

"I'll pass on living with the wolf and take door number two, please," I tell him, and he chuckles.

"Des isn't that bad."

I snort. "Are we talking about the same person here?" Desmond Pierce very much is that bad. He gets under my skin in a way no one else can, and the pull he has over me, urgh. I hate it. Sometimes so much so that I think I hate *him*. When we're in the same room, I want to kiss him and punch him in the same breath. It drives the tigress in me crazy, which in and of itself is infuriating. She shouldn't be drawn to him. I keep telling myself it's because he's hunter-born. Because he's strong and capable and a wolf above even Alpha's. That's why my tiger wants to slash at him and purr all at once, but the human in me knows he's an asshole and to stay far-the-fuck away.

Zheng gives me a light-hearted shove. "Alright, sis, have it your way. But don't come crying to me when you realize the grass isn't greener on the other side."

A gust of wind blows my hair into my face and I hastily push my black curls out of my eyes. "I won't," I assure him. "The grass on your side is already dead and yellow so the bar is set pretty low."

He smiles, his eyes scanning past me, and I turn to see a familiar black Escalade roll up beside my mother's car. The broody asshole I just mentioned parks his overpriced SUV and three doors open, letting out Des, Rafael, and Jordy.

Somebody please shoot me now.

"What are they doing here?" I groan.

Zheng throws his arm over my shoulder, the smell of black cardamom and mint falling like a comforting blanket over me as he pulls me into a side embrace. "They're being good friends and helping you move into your new place." The fact that he genuinely believes that should be concerning. Rose-colored glasses, anyone?

"Whose idea was this?" I ask with an unintended snarl in my voice.

Already their presence is drawing curious looks from some of the girls. It won't take long for them to realize who and what they are. God dammit, he is such an asshole. It would have been bad enough if he came on his own, but bringing Rafael and Jordy is taking it one step too far. Human girls go crazy for these assholes. I swear it's some weird shifter fetish, but they get even worse once they realize they play Infernum. There's talk of it becoming a national league game, televised and everything, so the guys who play in college have like this, celebrity status almost.

"Des's," Zheng confirms what I suspected, and my mother being the weirdo she is, gushes, because why wouldn't she? He's our Pack Hunter which makes him *soooo* special.

"Isn't that so sweet of them, Meiying? It makes me so happy to know you'll have such a great support system here. Makes me feel so much better about my baby girl going to college." She sighs, the smile on her face wistful as she turns back to the house. If I grind my teeth any harder, I'm liable to break a tooth. She cannot be serious right now.

"Yep. Soooo sweet," I tell her while giving Desmond my most murderous glare. Does he shake in fear like he should? Of course not. Instead his eyes flash with his wolf and he smirks like the cruel bastard he is and heads right for me, Rafael and Jordy right on his heels.

I'm going to make him regret this. I cannot believe he'd set me up like this.

The guys do that guy handshake bro hug thing as if they didn't all see each other a few hours ago, then Des turns his full attention on me, and I have to force my expression to remain impassive. Age has only worked to sharpen his features, making him even more striking than the boy I used to look at from afar when we were just kids in the Pack.

With his hair tightly braided away from his face, his sharp jawline and full lips stand out in stark relief, and I can't decide if I want to kiss him or punch him—a frequent struggle of mine, so I do what I'm best at and just antagonize him.

"Are you so desperate for female attention that you have to drop in on the girls of Kappa Eagle for a little bit of an ego stroke?" I smile in satisfaction when his dark brown eyes narrow, his eyes flashing silver.

Desmond has this edge to him that's difficult to describe. He's both regal and rugged; the juxtaposition between the two is likely what makes women flock to him. He has two thin slashes in his right brow that somehow take him from attractive to dangerous, and after graduation he filled out to a full six-foot-five, stacked with all the muscles you'd expect a shifter male to have. The effect he has on people is hard to miss.

When he scowls the way he is doing right now, he's damn near terrifying to behold. It makes your flight or fight instinct rise up and a small part of you suddenly feels like prey. But when he smiles, a real smile that doesn't hold an ounce of malice—and mind you those are rare—his entire face lights up, and for a second it's like standing in the sun after months of nothing but rain.

*God, I hate him.*

"I don't need an ego stroke. Not a single woman here can hold my interest," he says, his eyes boring into mine and waiting for a reaction. One I refuse to deliver. *Asshole.* Of course he'd say something like that. Desmond hasn't dated, like seriously dated, for as long as I've known him. He gets around, I'm sure. Shifters don't bat an eye when it comes to skin privileges. We're tactile creatures, and our beasts crave simple comforts. But the only girl I've seen him with more than once is Tamara Vinzent. I haven't had the pleasure of meeting her yet. She's a wolf so I've seen her in passing, but we've never spoken, and she's always his date to any event or function that requires one. I don't really understand their relationship, and for my own sanity, I try not to think about it too much, but somehow she's outlasted everyone else and has managed to sink some sortof a hold into Desmond where no others before her have succeeded.

When Desmond realizes I'm not going to respond, the corner of his mouth curls into his signature cruel smile. "You worried someone will catch my attention?" He scans the growing crowd. "Not really my type, but maybe I can—"

"Yo, Baby Liu," Jordy says, cutting Desmond off from whatever he was about to say and cutting through the growing tension in the air. "You gonna show us the new digs? Introduce us to your new lady friends?" He winks, and if I didn't know him better, I'd think he was serious. But Jordy is head over heels in love with his Joaninha, one of my best friends, so I know this is for show and he's just helping me out. The softy. Too bad his little act of kindness won't keep him safe if he and the others don't get the hell out of here before anyone realizes the school's star Infernum players just showed up.

I shake my head. "Hard no. You three need to leave."

Rafael smirks and Jordy clutches his heart as though I just wounded him. "Baby L—"

"Stop calling me that and go home or I'm going to tell Jo about your big surprise," I warn.

He sucks in a sharp breath. "You wouldn't. You love me?" He meant it as a statement, but it comes out more as a question.

"Wanna bet?" Because today is day one of campus life for me and I'm not going to let these three muck it up.

Jordy backs away, hands raised in the air. "You win. I'll stay in the car." He turns and jogs back to Des's Escalade. One down. Two more to go.

I turn to Rafael and raise a single brow. "You too, wolf."

"You don't have anything you can use against me," he says, his voice filled with confidence he should not be feeling right now. Doesn't he know me? I have something on virtually everyone. It's little sister 101. You always find the dirt and horde it to later get your way.

I prop one hand on my hip. "I don't?" I press a finger to my lips as though thinking before letting a wide smile spread across my face. "Hey, Zheng, did I ever tell you about the time Rafael and Isa went to Silverdale?"

Rafael's eyes widen briefly before his brows draw together. "How do you—"

I pull my phone from my back pocket. "Isa sent me pictures from that weekend. You two were so cute together. The couples—"

Rafael jerks forward with a snarl, pressing his palm over my mouth. His dark brown eyes fill with a mix of disbelief and fury. "Not. Another. Word," he growls. If he were anybody else, I might be worried by the threat in his voice, but despite his rough exterior, Rafael is a big ole softie and his fiancé is one of my other best friends. He wouldn't hurt a hair on my head. She loves me. He loves her.

Therefore, I win. So instead of pushing his hand away or trying to say anything, I wait for him to realize what I already know.

It takes only a handful of seconds.

"Fine. Don't say anything else. I'll go chill with Jordy. Deal?"

I nod and he slowly releases me, hesitating for just a second to make sure I'll keep my mouth shut before he turns, slaps Des on the shoulder with a muttered, "You're on your own, man," and joins Jordy in the car.

"Damn, sis, remind me not to get on your bad side," Zheng says, as if I haven't used this exact same tactic on him before. "Got anything on this one?" He nods toward Desmond, who raises a brow of his own, expression smug because, no, I have nothing I can use against him to make him do anything he doesn't want to do and he knows it.

# Chaper Two

## Desmond

I smile, watching the gears turn in that pretty little head of hers as she struggles to find a way to get rid of me. Not happening, kitten. Meiying coming to Hellbound U is a disaster waiting to happen. She's seventeen for chrissakes, and her idiot mother thought it'd be a great idea for her to join the mixed faction sorority campus. What a joke. Pack members might be required to attend Hellbound U, but Clan Wolf keeps its female pack mates in tight units and well protected. I know Meiying is capable, but the idea of her being here, alone and away from the Pack, sets the wolf in me on edge.

It's become a habit of mine to avoid the frats and sororities. I go to my classes, put in my time for Infernum, and focus on Pack business. I don't have time for anything else. But only a hermit wouldn't know Kappa Eagle and their frat counterpart, Alpha Ze, are the two most notorious party houses here. Problem is, when shit goes down, it gets ugly. These aren't your typical houses. They're packed full of druids, witches, fae, and all manner of paranormals. It's not just booze you have to worry about, which would be a non-issue since shifter metabolism processes alcohol too quickly to get drunk. But now you have to worry about potions and magicked drugs engineered for paranormal genetics.

There have been plenty of rumors about girls getting drugged and guys taking turns at some of their parties, and I'll be damned if anyone is going to try shit like that with Meiying.

I can't stand the girl, but that doesn't mean I'll sit back and let anything happen to her, either. She's Pack, and I'm not a complete asshole, despite what she might think.

It's why I suggested to Zheng that she move in with us. I'm willing to take one for the team if I have to, not that it'd be some big hardship. I'm barely home during the week. Most of my time is spent in class, on the field, or at the Compound, and most weekends I have games. Half of them being out of town.

I'm home most Sunday afternoons but generally gone in the evening to see my sister. Sundays are the obligatory Pierce family dinners. My parents made them mandatory when KeAnna and I moved out for college, and while I managed to find a way out of them, my sister wasn't so lucky. She goes to school out of state and she still has to fly in for those fucking dinners, so I make it a point to at least catch up with her while she's here and take her to the airport for her return flight whenever I can.

Where Meiying and Zheng's parents are damn near absent, mine take overbearing to an entirely different level.

Zheng liked the idea of Meiying moving in. He's protective of his little sister the same way I am of mine, so it should have been a done deal, except Meiying refused to get on board with the program. The pretty little idiot.

When she shot down the idea, there wasn't shit I could do about it, and Zheng wasn't willing to pressure her. Something about her being independent and responsible and yeah, compared to most female shifters her age, maybe she is. But she's still young. Impressionable. Guys are going to take one look at her small body, perfect tits, and seductive mouth and think she's theirs for the taking. Wolves don't let their females leave the den this young and on their own. I have no fucking idea why the cats would. It's stupid and dangerous as hell. I know shit seems smooth between factions now, but that can change any minute. We're always teetering on the edge of war. It's too ingrained in our nature to see the other factions, especially the vampires, as anything but enemies.

"Why are you here?" she asks like she doesn't already know.

"I'm helping. That's what *friens* do." I put more emphasis on the word friend than necessary, but sometimes I need to remind myself that's what we're supposed to be. Friends. Not enemies. Not rivals. She's part of my Pack even if we're not in the same Clan, and even more, she's part of our crew, which means I'm obligated to look out for her the same as I would for Isa and Joaninha—Rafael and Jordy's girls.

But fuck, the way she gets under my skin, sometimes it's all I can do not to spank her ass to get her to behave. Meiying Liu is a match just waiting to be lit, and I'm the spark that gets the tigress in her roaring. The way we verbally spar with one another, her tongue like a whip intent on tearing me down, it makes my cock jerk just thinking about how she'd be in the sack. Would she be just as wild and unrestrained? Or would she be shy and submissive? Would her beast submit to my wolf?

Unlikely. *Get your shit together, D.* I fight the urge to adjust myself and force my face to remain impassive. I'm not interested. Not really. I'm also not blind. Meiying's all grown up. Her waist dips beneath her ribs, giving her an hourglass figure that should be illegal on a seventeen-year-old girl. Her tits are full and round and her ass is more than a handful that I've definitely considered squeezing a time or two. Again, not because I'm interested.

I lock down thoughts like that as soon as they occur. Meiying Liu is one hundred percent off limits. For one, she is too fucking young. Four years might not seem like a big deal to everyone else, but it sure as shit is when the girl in question is a minor. And for two, I don't do relationships.

Between school, Infernum, and Pack duties, I don't have time for one, nor am I particularly fond of having someone all up in my business. Women are needy and temperamental, shifters more so than humans. If the urge arises, I'll find a girl to take home for the night to share skin privileges with, but that's all I'm interested in. One night. I'm not looking for a mate.

Besides, I'm pretty sure Zheng would have my balls if I made a play for her. There's an unspoken rule between friends. Thou shall not fuck one another's siblings.

He and I are damn near brothers at this point. No way can I cross that line.

After graduation, the plan was for Rafael, Jordy, and I to get a place together. But both fuckers had to go and couple up senior year of high school, so that plan went down the drain real quick and left me with two options. Move into the dorms—not fucking likely—or get my own place. But then money would be tight and I didn't want to ask my parents to cover it. Doing that would lead to trouble. Nothing given was ever given freely, and I didn't want the strings I knew would be attached. On top of that, my wolf would revolt. Wolves are Pack animals. We don't do well in isolation, so having my own place would have irritated my beast over time.

But the idea of living with a stranger isn't something I could get on board with, so I buried my shit with Zheng and got a place with him since the fucker was the only other one in our crew riding solo like myself.

Since he and the girls are all close, it made sense, even if he is a cat. We weren't going to be getting rid of him anytime soon. And looking back, it was the right call, even if I didn't love the idea at the time.

Zheng's good people. He fucked up when we were all kids, but since then, when any of us need him, he shows up. He's there when it counts, and he's put his ass on the line for me more times than I can count. I won't repay that by banging his sister behind his back, even if there was that one time we kissed, and it still fucking haunts me.

*"You goo•, man?" Rafael asks.*

*I grunt, refusing to take my eyes off the girl in front of me, my wolf instincts* riding me hard as a growl works its way up my throat. "Fucking peachy."

Rafael snorts and places his hand on my shoulder.

"Right. Well, while you pine over baby Liu, I'm gonna go get my girl before Jordy tries to steal her."

"I'm not pining," I retort. I don't pine after chicks, least of all a cat with too much sass and too little sense. What the fuck does she think she's doing right now? And where the hell is her brother. Shouldn't he be watching her or something? At the very least, he should be fending off the assholes who just want to take advantage of her. No way would I let guys be all over my sister like that.

He laughs, shaking his head. "Call it whatever you want, but your jealousy is showing, man. Might want to get that in check."

I grind my teeth together, flipping off his retreating back. Rafe doesn't know what he's talking about. Baby Liu isn't anything special. A piece of ass and soon to be jailbait. Not someone I'd be jealous over.

Speaking of Liu's, Zheng walks up beside me and hands me a Coke. I accept the drink, knowing the fucker is just being nice, and against my better judgement I ask, "You cool with older guys from other Clans all over your baby sister?" I feign indifference and take a drink of the soda, waiting to see how he reacts. It has nothing to do with wondering if the age difference between her and I would matter to him and everything to do with making sure he knows what's going on with Meiying right now.

As expected, Zheng follows my gaze. His eyes narrow and he mutters a curse. "Shit. I'll have to drag her away from a fucking harem and I'll have to deal with her snarling about it the entire way home today."

I force a laugh. "She's a handful."

He shakes his head. "That's putting it mildly. I don't know what her deal is, man. Lately, it's like she's looking for trouble." He sighs. "I better go deal with that."

I thrust a hand out to stop him. "Let me." I don't know why I make the suggestion, but I don't try to walk it back once it's out there.

His dark brows pull together. "You sure, man?"

I nod. "Yeah. Let her be pissed at me. Then on the way home when she's bitching you can pretend to agree with what an asshole I am."

He gives me a feline smirk and slaps me on the back. "Thanks, man. I owe you one." I nod like it's no big deal. Just helping the guy out. I don't have a single selfish reason for making the suggestion.

Isa calls his name and Zheng turns. "Go," I tell him. "I'll get it handled."

He hesitates for a moment. "You sure, man? Meiying can be—"

I cut him off. "Bro, I've got it. Go see what Isa wants." He walks away, heading toward Rafael and Isa on the other side of the yard, and without missing a beat, I head straight toward my prey. She's got herself surrounded by some of Isa's friends from back home. I met the guys earlier, Damian, Kai, and Josué. They seem nice enough, but that doesn't mean any of them should be talking to her right now.

I pick up on their conversation with my heightened hearing and slow my steps, casually walking closer to the group. Damian, who's on her right, is laying it on thick. He's smiling at her like she's all that he sees.

Not happening, asshole.

As soon as I'm behind her, I pull her back into my chest and wrap my arms around her, pinning her in place with her back to my front. I ignore the way she feels pressed up against me and focus on the miscreants in front of me.

Meiying doesn't bother trying to twist to see who's grabbed her. If my scent didn't give me away, my dark arms banded around her is telling enough. I'm the only black guy here. She doesn't have to see my face to know it's me, and being the smart girl she is, she doesn't bother putting up a fight to get away.

"You know Baby Liu is jailbait, right?" I direct the question first to Damian before making eye contact with the other two. Meiying stiffens in my arms and a beautiful shade of pink creeps up her neck as a low growl vibrates in her throat.

"For you, maybe," Damian retorts with a shrug.

The corner of Josué's mouth lifts into a smirk, like he's in on some secret, but he doesn't say anything. He takes a drink of his soda and rocks back on his heels, watching things play out. Kai, on the other hand, gives a hard shake of his head. "Ain't no one trying to tap that," he says. "We're all friends. Just having a conversation. No one's crossing any lines."

Damian snorts. "Speak for yourself," he tells him, and then looks Meiying right in the eyes. "I have no problem saying I am very much interested." He licks his lips and gives her a heated look that makes me want to punch the fucker in the face. "Wanna blow this place? Go have some fun?" I can smell the lust on him and it's taking everything in me not to shift and tear into the asshole.

I can't see Meiying's expression, but if I had to guess she's probably eating this shit up, if only to irritate me more. But her scent hasn't shifted like his. She still smells like oranges and ginseng, without any trace of desire.

"Why not?" I can hear the smile in her voice.

"She's fourteen," I grind out.

"I'm seventeen. Age is just a number, man." He shrugs. "Besides, skin *privileges are no big deal. Stop being such a tight-ass, man. You're worse than the maternals."*

*Meiying squirms in my arms in an attempt to get away, but I shift her around, putting her firmly behind me before stepping up and getting in Damian's face with a low and threatening growl. "She's too young for you, so knock that shit off. No guy here is going to let you put the moves on Liu's little sister."*

*Despite having to look up to meet my stare, Damian doesn't back down. "Did it sound like I was asking for permission?" I let my wolf bleed into my eyes and his beast rises up in challenge, but I'm something this asshole didn't expect.*

*Less than two seconds pass before he curses and looks away, but rather than leaving it there, he takes a deep breath and tries to level me with his stare again. My wolf snarls and rakes its claws against my flesh, eager to put this pup in his place, but before I do anything that will land me on Isa's shit list, like beating her friend to a pulp when I've already proven I'm the more dominant of the two of us, I wait for him to avert his gaze again and then turn on my heel.*

*I grab Meiying by the arm, pulling her with me as I go. "Desmond, let go of me," she complains, but her steps follow. A glance over my shoulder shows Josué with a hand against Damian's chest while he mutters something in his ear. Whatever it is he's saying, it keeps him in place, and that's good enough for me. Kid's still growing into himself and his instincts are riding high, but they're pushing him in the wrong direction, which is towards a fight with me he has no chance of winning.*

*I drag Meiying around the side of the house where no one can see us and press her up against the brick exterior, my arms caging her in on either side and offering her zero chance of escape.*

*Does she look worried? Not one fucking bit. The girl looks pissed and ready to raise hell.*

"What is your problem! You had no right—" she snarls, her tigress rising up in her gaze as she shoves against my chest, but despite her shifter strength, it's like a kitten swatting at a bull. I barely feel it. "You can't manhandle me like that. You are not my keeper. And you do not get to dictate who I hang out with."

"I have every right," I grind out the words and her eyes flare. Shit. I didn't mean for that to come out. The girl gets in my head. Under my skin. She is so goddamn infuriating.

"What is it exactly that gives you the—"

*No answer is a good answer, so instead, I close the distance between us and capture her lips with my own to shut her up. At least that's what I tell myself. She jumps, but I don't let that deter me. I step forward into her space, pressing my mouth more firmly against her own and deepening the kiss while grabbing her beneath her thighs and lifting her into my arms. Her legs wrap around my waist instinctively and I press her back against the house. A small moan passes across her lips and I want to hear it again, so I press my hardening cock against her jean-clad center and grind my hips against hers.*

*She gasps, tearing her mouth away and sucking in a lungful of air. I nip at her full lips and trail kisses down her jawline. Her neck. All while thrusting my hips against her, letting her feel how badly I want her right now.*

"What are you doing?" she asks with jagged breath.

*I don't answer. Instead, I capture her lips again and drink down her soft sighs and sweet moans. If I were being honest with her, I'd say I had no fucking clue what I was doing, but as soon as I open my mouth to speak, all of this stops, an• I'm not rea•y for that to happen just yet.*

I shake out the memories from that day and focus back on the here and now.

"We're not friends," Meiying retorts, arms folded across her chest and mouth pressed into a tight line.

I shrug like her words don't affect me.

"We're not even friendly," she adds.

She's not wrong. Since that kiss, shit between us has gone from bad to worse. Meiying and I are like cats and dogs, or oil and water. We don't mix. When we do, things get heated and not in a good way. It's my fault for the way things are between us, and I'm man enough to own that, but when I pressed my mouth against hers and swallowed her soft cries of pleasure I knew right away it was a mistake.

"I'm friends with him." I nod in Zheng's direction. "And I'd be a shit friend if I didn't at least offer to help the guy out. We both know he'll do most of the heavy lifting while you and your mom talk with whoever is running this show."

Her nostrils flare and I can tell she's barely keeping herself in check. I love it when she gets like this. All fire and brimstone, ready to raise hell to get what she wants. But before she can say anything else, her mom tugs on her arm. "Meiying, leave the poor boy alone. He's only trying to help." She tugs on her daughter's arm, who reluctantly follows, throwing one last look my way before admitting defeat.

I give her a small wave and her eyes narrow even further. She'll come up with a way to get me back.

I'm looking forward to it.

# Chaper Three

## Meiying

I hate him. I hate him. I hate him. I repeat the mantra a dozen times in my head until I convince myself it's the truth. Why does he have to be so infuriating all of the time? My tiger rakes her claws beneath my flesh, though not in an angry way. She's intrigued by the stupid wolf, though why, I have no idea.

Mom doesn't give me long to dwell on it before she marches me right through the front doors and to the left down a long hallway. We pass a living room, dining room, and kitchen before coming to the open door of an office with a small gold placard that reads, "Housemother."

"Knock, knock," my mother calls before stepping inside, pulling me right along with her.

An attractive brunette looks up and greets us, a wide smile on her face. "You must be Mrs. Liu?" she says, coming around her desk and shaking mom's hand.

"Ms. Douglas, actually. Meiying's father and I divorced years ago." She throws this out with a laugh like it's no big deal, but I know mom hates it. Dad forced her to change her name after the divorce. Said she didn't deserve it and the perks that came with being a Liu. He's an asshole and whatever perks come with my name, I'm still waiting on to be delivered, but he's also my dad, so I'm duty bound to love him. Even when he's absent and downright cruel where mom is concerned. "But please, call me Helen."

"Nice to meet you, Helen. I'm Hilary, the Kappa Eagle president." She says this with a sugary sweet smile so wide her cheeks are bound to crack. She's not much older than I am. Twenty-one or twenty-two, if I had to guess. She smells like sage and lavender and I immediately peg her for a witch. "And you must be Meiying, our newest shifter recruit. We are so excited to have you."

I'll bet she is. She might be fooling Mom, but the fake smile and high-pitched laugh is not fooling me.

"Thanks," I tell her, accepting her offered hand with a fake smile of my own.

"Hills, we're out of—" A girl says behind us but cuts herself off when she sees Hilary isn't alone. "Oh. My bad. I didn't realize you were meeting with parents today," the girl adds almost sheepishly. Her scent is similar to Hilary's, though a note sweeter, so she's likely a witch as well.

I spot the empty liquor bottles in both her hands and know right away what they've recently run out of. I chance a look at my mom, curious to see how she'll react, but her smile is wide, her eyes glazed over, as though she's reliving fond memories before she lets out a little laugh.

"Please, don't worry about me. You girls do what you need to. Are you over twenty-one?" Mom asks her.

"Oh, umm, I ..." She turns to Hilary with wide eyes and a *help me* expression.

Mom laughs again. "Why don't I do you girls a favor and make a quick trip to the store while you guys show my baby girl around. That looks like," she tilts her head for a better look at the bottles the newcomer is clearly trying and failing to hide, "Rum, Vodka, and ... is that schnapps?"

The girl nods but keeps her lips sealed.

"Perfect. I'll be back in a jiff."

Mom brushes a kiss across my temple and then slips past the girl and leaves me standing alone with two very surprised college girls.

"Did your mom just—"

"Offer to go buy you booze after you very obviously failed to confirm that you're legally old enough to drink? Yes. Yes, she did."

"Wicked. Your mom is so cool."

I sigh and force myself to smile. "We're shifters. Our bodies metabolize alcohol too quickly to get more than a mild buzz so she doesn't consider it an issue like most adults would. I'm Meiying by the way."

"Quinn," the girl says. "Nice to meet you."

"Let's show you around and go over the house rules while we wait for your mom to get back," Hilary interjects. "Quinn, why don't you go make sure the other pledges don't need any assistance."

Quinn nods and leaves to do what Hilary asked, and when I turn to face her, her smile is gone and an annoyed expression rests in its place. "Look," she begins. "I'm going to be honest. I wasn't thrilled when I was told we'd be admitting a new pledge. You skipped our entire application process, didn't show up for a single interview, and didn't have to jump through any of the hoops every other girl who was accepted had to."

I keep my expression blank. Is she wanting me to apologize for something I played zero part in and had no control over? It's not like I asked for this.

She sighs. "But, you're part of the Pack and our house takes that seriously. We need shifters to be involved and you're the only one who's considered joining. It also doesn't hurt that your dad made a donation to Kappa Eagle in your name." Huh, look at that. Good ole Dad helping us out. I try not to roll my eyes. He was probably worried I'd ask to live with him full time, what with mom leaving. Not that I ever would. I love my dad, but where Mom parents by trying to be my friend, Dad parents with assistants and nannies, forgetting I'm seventeen, not seven, and that I'd do better defending and watching over him than he ever could watch over me.

"So, we're going to make this work." She sounds resigned. Join the club. " Hanging out with high schoolers isn't really our thing but like I said, your shifter status makes you the exception. We also don't want any trouble with the dean's office for exposing you to anything you're not ready for, so for now, keep your age to yourself. You don't look as young as you are, so that will work in our favor."

I snort. Pretty sure she won't expose me to anything I haven't been exposed to already. Shifters aren't shy or meek by any means.

We like to experience life to the fullest, and that includes pushing any and all boundaries and getting into trouble on the regular, but I keep that to myself.

"I can do that," I tell her. It's not like I was planning on announcing my age, anyway.

"Good. Glad that's out of the way. Like the plaque outside the door says, I'm the housemother, but I'm not going to be your mom while you're here. If you're upset or homesick, phone a friend. I'm not your shoulder to cry on."

"Noted."

"And I'm not your babysitter. The girls here like to have a bit of fun and we're close with some of the campus fraternities. You're responsible for looking after yourself. If you can't handle your liquor, don't drink. And if you do drink, don't be stupid and drive yourself home. Got it?"

I give her two thumbs up and decided not to remind her that I can't get drunk. I hate repeating myself. "Anything else?"

"Don't cut classes. Part of eligibility requirements for being a member is maintaining a 3.0 GPA. If you fail any of your classes, you're out. Shifter or not."

"Good to know."

She reaches behind her and grabs an envelope from her desk before handing it to me. "Inside is a map of campus, our events schedule, and your school ID. You're required to attend all Kappa Eagle functions so add these dates to your calendar. We don't make exceptions."

I tuck the envelope in the back pocket of my jeans. "Okay." Not like I have a packed social calendar or anything. I hang out with Isa and Joaninha on most weekends, but we don't generally plan anything official. It's usually just junk food and movies while the guys lock themselves in the media room to watch videos of past Infernum games. They're a little obsessed.

If I have a sorority thing, no one will care if I need to skip a night.

"Your room is on the first floor toward the back of the house. It's just you and Quinn, the girl you just met, on this level. Everyone else is upstairs. There's a back entrance near your room you can use if you need to and additional parking out back if you have a car." I nod. My dad bought me a WRX like Zheng's, only mine is candy apple red, as a *'congrats you're going to college'* gift, so that will be convenient. He's supposed to have his driver deliver it sometime this week, so I'll have to let him know they can bring it straight here. It'll save me from needing a campus parking pass since I really only plan on driving when I need to go off campus or go to the Compound.

I walk everywhere else.

"If you have questions, check with Quinn first. All of our new recruits are assigned a big sister. She's yours."

I nod. "Okay. Cool." Do I leave now? I'm not sure what protocol is here exactly. Should I wait to be excused?

"That's it," Hilary confirms with a huff.

"Great. Thanks." I make a hasty retreat and wander around downstairs, ducking around the other girls in the house until I find a long hallway that leads to the back. I figure I'll get to know everyone later. Right now I just want to track down my room and unpack.

The first door I find is decorated with pictures and drawings. I make a wild guess that it's Quinn's, since it's her face in most of the pictures. Further down the hall are two more doors. One at the very end, which I confirm is the door that leads outside. I open it to find a small patch of grass and a concrete slab for parking on my right that leads to the main road.

I close that door and turn to the last one, which I'm assuming is mine. I find Zheng lounging on my bed, phone in hand, and take in the rest of the space. It's a decent size. Double closet. I scan the room for Desmond, noting the pile of neatly stacked boxes next to the bed, half expecting him to burst from behind them just to fuck with me, but his scent in the room is light, barely there. Why does that bother me?

"Where's Des?" I ask when it's clear my brother isn't going to volunteer the information, too distracted by whoever he's texting with on his phone.

"His coach called. The guys had to leave for some Infernum team thing."

Relief sweeps through me and my shoulders sag. I plop down on the bed beside my brother. "I see you found my room?"

He nods, setting his phone aside. "Yeah, one of the girls told us which one was yours, so we moved all your stuff in for you."

"Rafael and Jordy didn't wait in the car, did they?"

He gives me a crooked grin. "Nope."

"Urgh," I groan, hiding my face with my hands. "Did anyone recognize them?"

Zheng chuckles. "Relax, sis. All they saw were some stacked guys moving boxes. No one asked if they were on the team, or wolves, or any of that shit, though Jordy definitely got his fair share of phone numbers."

I scowl. "He better have thrown them away." Jordy is a notorious flirt, but also absolutely obsessed with Jo, his girlfriend and the mother of his child. They're doing really well, but I know Joaninha sometimes has a hard time with all the attention Jordy receives. And being an Infernum player doesn't help. I swear all of the guys have their own personal fan clubs now.

Zheng leans forward and tugs open the drawer of a nearby nightstand. Five small pieces of paper with girly handwriting in various colors greet me. "Nah, he left them for you so you could make friends. His words, not mine."

I don't bother fighting the smile that spreads over my face. That sounds like Jordy, alright.

Zheng leaves a few minutes later with the promise to help me find my classes on Monday when school starts. "Call me if you need me," he tells me on his way out, giving me a quick hug, and I breathe in my brother's scent.

"I will," I promise, and then settle in and unpack my things. The room is a blank canvas. White walls, hardwood floors, and a single window that gives me a glimpse of where my car will soon be parked. There's a queen bed, a single nightstand, and a tall dresser, but nothing else aside from my boxes of belongings. I unpack my clothes first, hanging up what needs to be hung and folding everything else to add to the dresser drawers.

Mom shows up later that afternoon, her arms loaded down with shopping bags and a wide smile on her face.

"What is all that?" I ask, eyeing the pops of pink and gold peeking out the tops of the bags. I'm not a tomboy, but I'm not really a girly girl either. I generally go for comfort over style.

"Paranormal Barn was next to the grocery store, so I thought I'd pick up a few things you might need. Wait until you see the comforter set I got you," she gushes, pulling out a white down comforter decorated with small pink tassels around the edge and dotted with gold stars.

"Pretty," I deadpan. I'm not sure what the purpose of the tassels is, but it could have been worse.

"I know, right? I wanted to make sure you were all set. I can't believe my little girl is all grown up and going to college. I know this is a big step, but I want you to know I am so proud of you."

"Thanks, Mom."

She beams. "Let's get you settled. I only have an hour before I need to get on the road, but that's plenty of time for us to turn this room into your home for the next four years."

I groan. Four years. She really expects me to be a sorority girl for all four years of college?

Her eyes soften. "I know being a Kappa Eagle might not seem exciting to you right now, but honey, you're going to love it. You're going to meet new people and make friends you never would have had the chance to meet had you stayed in the Compound. Try to be open-minded."

I sigh. "I'll try."

"Now, let's get this room situated."

# Chaper Four

## Desmond

Rafael takes off down the field and I lunge for the fifty-pound silver sphere hurtling my way before I slingshot it in his direction, the cool metal burns my hands as soon as I make contact with it, but I'm quick to release it, not holding it for a second longer than I have to.

The ball whistles through the air, heading straight for Rafael. He jumps up into the air to catch it and it collides with his chest. He lets out a whoop of laughter as his feet touch back on the ground, followed by a string of curses as he races up the field, but is forced to drop the ball when he's less than ten yards away.

"Dammit." I kick the turf and tear off my helmet, frustration coursing through me. Infernum is set to showcase not only every faction's strengths, but also their weaknesses, and silver is a big fat weakness of ours. The balls are selected at random. Up to three are on the field at any given time, and the silver ones are making it damn near impossible for us to win a game lately.

Rafael jerks to a stop before lunging forward to salvage the pass. He manages to retrieve the ball with both hands, tucking it against his chest before running again and crossing past the goal line, but it costs him.

As soon as he's clear, he drops the ball, his wolf snarling in pain as his skin visibly trembles with his urge to shift, something we're not allowed to do on the field.

"Not bad, man." I call out to him.

"That was shit and you know it."

I offer a noncommittal shrug. "Progress at least. You held it longer than you did in last week's game."

"True enough," he sighs.

Rafael plays wolfback so he's expected to score more than anyone else, which is why building up a silver tolerance is crucial. Coach called me in for an emergency meeting, worried about my ability to throw the damn things, though that doesn't seem to be our main issue. I dropped Jordy off on the way, but Rafael decided to tag along. Good thing too, because he needs the practice as much as I do.

"You could always sit this next one out," I offer, but he shakes his head.

"You know I can't." Our second string wolfback—Deacon Hunt—is a freshman and a Fae. The guy can throw, but he's from one of the high courts and isn't used to being punched in the face. Something that happens regularly on the field in Infernum. Under normal circumstances, I wouldn't care. The point of bringing him on board is to train with him, get him where he needs to be, so that by the time I graduate next year, he's ready. He's got potential and he needs the field time if he's going to grow, but next week Rafael's pops—my Alpha—is coming, and we need to make him proud.

If word gets out that we're struggling to hold the fucking ball for a few seconds, our strength and dominance will come into question. It's just a game, but at the same time, it isn't. As the Pack Hunter there are certain expectations that've been thrust upon me, and as the Alpha Heir, there are a shit ton more that've been heaped on Rafe.

Neither of us will be the reason our team loses. Not when we're playing Moonbound U, a mostly vampire led team. And no way is either of us going to let a fucking Fae lead our team to glory.

"Let's go again," I tell Rafael and he nods, getting into position. But before he starts, a voice from the sidelines draws our attention.

"Pierce!" Coach yells. "What the hell do you think you're doing?"

I grind my teeth together and wait as he stalks across the field like a bull. Barely six feet and thick around the middle, it's been a hot minute since the man was in his prime, but he still has no problem going toe to toe with any one of us. Damn Druid. When he's within earshot without me needing to yell, I tell him, "Practicing, Coach."

"Practicing what, exactly? I gave you explicit orders—"

"We need to build up a tolerance," I tell him. "We won't win if we wince every time we touch the damn ball."

His brows pull together and I know he wants to fight me on it, but he wants a win against Moonbound U as badly as we do.

"Silver burns are no joke, son. If you don't take care of your hands, you'll permanently scar. You need to shift between plays. Let your wolf have a chance to heal you between injuries so you don't create any permanent damage."

I grunt. "Can't do that during a game," I remind him.

He takes off his red Hellbound U baseball cap and shakes his head. "No. Which is why you should make sure to do it now."

I grind my teeth together but nod, knowing he's right. "Fine. We'll shift between plays."

Rafael nods in agreement and Coach exhales a relieved breath before rubbing his jaw. "How's your hand feel when you throw?"

Like lava being poured on it, but I keep that to myself. "It stings, but I can handle it."

He considers me for a moment. "And your beast?"

"We're in control." Rafael answers for me.

Coach works his jaw. "Alright. Fine. But you know the rules."

"A loss of control means you forfeit the game. We know. Neither of us is at risk of shifting unless we want to."

He nods to himself. "Alright. I'll leave you two to it then. Make sure you check in with the healers at the day's end. Got it?"

I grit my teeth at the order, but nod. Coach is an alright guy and doesn't understand shifter dominance, so I fight my instincts to put him in his place. He puts the players' health and well-being first, and I have no doubt he'll bench me and any other shifter if we don't take him seriously.

"Good. We'll make this work. But, if we get too many silver balls in next week's game…" he trails off and yeah. We get it. "You prepared to take that risk?"

I nod. I understand Infernum is just a game, but it's more than that too. My parents hate that I play. They think it's beneath me, but my Alpha won't let them keep me from playing. It brings too much pride to the Pack to see us not only play, but dominate, so this isn't one of those scenarios where they can trample all over what I want to do. I'm hunter-born, which comes with its own set of expectations, but on the field, I can avoid the doom and gloom of my fate, which is a lonely existence where even those in my clan are on edge when in my presence. It comes with the territory when you're born to play the part of grim reaper to any Pack mate who has the misfortune of going rogue.

So no, I won't give this up. Not for my parents and not because of my aversion to silver. If the vampires can manage to play when balls of fire are thrown about, I sure as hell can manage this. "It's worth the risk, Coach."

"Have it your way. Now get your asses home, shift, and get some rest."

Coach stalks off the field toward the locker room and we head the opposite direction toward the parking lot. "You good, man?" Rafael asks once we reach our vehicles and I clench my fists, waiting for the Lyc-V in my system to take root and start healing the damage on my palms. It's minor. Some soreness and discoloration, but more or an irritant than anything.

I look at Rafe and take in the blackened blisters on his hands and forearms. *Shit.*

"Pretty sure I should be asking you that."

"Nah, I'm good." He sucks on his teeth and hesitates like he's got something else to say, which isn't like him, so I spit out, "What?" Only to see his frown deepen.

"What was up this morning?"

"What do you mean?" I open my door and lean against the frame. I have a feeling I know where this is going, and I don't like it. Rafael is my friend, and pretty soon, he'll be my Alpha if he sticks on the path he's on now, but that doesn't mean I like him questioning me.

"With Baby Liu. If she'd asked us to help her move in, we would have. The girl's one of us but ..." he trails off and shakes his head, running a hand through his dark brown hair.

"You're reading too much into it," I tell him, hoping he drops it.

He doesn't. Nosy wolf. "Nah. I don't think I am. Where's your head at these days? I know you had a thing for her back in high school, but—"

I cut him off before he has a chance to finish. "It's not like that. She's Zheng's little sister."

Rafael snorts. "Which meant fuck all when we were in high school and you gawked at her ass every time she walked by. Dude, I scent your lust every time she walks in a room."

"Like I said, you're reading too much into it. That was three years ago. Things change, and it wasn't lust. Not for her.."

He snorts. "Bullshit. Meiying is all grown up and she's filled out in all the right places. Don't pretend you haven't noticed."

I lift a single brow. "Isa know you've been checking Meiying out?"

He chuckles. "No cabrón, because I'm not. But I'm not blind and neither are you. The girl has grown up. A lot. Tension with you two has always been thick, your beasts pushing you both to establish dominance, but lately ..." He trails off, giving me a knowing look.

I shake my head. "Nah, man. Things between us are not like that. I can barely stand the girl so, no, I don't fucking like her. Not the way you're suggesting. She's a fucking cat. You know how crazy they are. Whatever you're picking up on is just our usual shit. We get under each other's skin. That's all." I might have the occasional fantasy about fucking her to see if it would make her more tolerable, but I don't let my dick dictate my decisions.

"I was just helping Zheng out. You and Jordy didn't have to come," I add, needing to end this conversation before he gets any ideas.

He gives me an incredulous look. "Really? That's the bullshit you're gonna try and feed me right now? Like I can't smell that lie from here without even trying?"

"Drop it, man. I'm telling you, I'm not interested. Sue me. I get a kick out of riling the girl up. I saw an opportunity and I took it. That doesn't mean I want her." Though I wouldn't mind her on her knees for me, mouth open and—*Fuck. Drop that line of thinking before you get your ass in trouble.*

Rafael levels me with an incredulous look. "I'm one of your best friends, cabrón. I'm not buying what you're selling. I know you better than that and there—" He stabs a finger in my direction. "I smell you, asshole. Your lust is like fucking pheromones in the air, eagerly searching for your woman."

I let out a snarl. "Ro, she's just a kid, not even eighteen yet. And you know how I am with females. You really think I'm gonna fuck myself over by trying to get a piece of her?" I shake my head. "I'm not that dumb. Isa, Joaninha, and KeAnna would all have my balls if I fucked things up with Meiying."

"So don't fuck it up, then. Give shit a real try, bro. You two have been going at it since senior year. You know there's something there. Everyone else can see it. Why can't you?"

"Because there isn't anything to see."

His stare is penetrating, his wolf glaring at me in challenge as I wait for him to concede the point. Rafe is dominant, but I'm hunter-born, which means even his gaze doesn't affect me, so I refuse to give in.

"Is this because of Zheng?" he asks. "You know he'd come around."

"No, fucker. This is because of me. What part of 'I'm not interested' do you not understand?" He opens his mouth to argue, but I cut him off. "I don't want hearts and rainbows with any female, let alone Meiying-fucking-Liu, okay? You're wifed up and I'm happy for you, man. For Jordy too. But I'm only interested in a tight piece of ass and a hot lay and Meiying isn't who I plan on getting that from." I make my words especially crude, hoping he gets the point. "So stop pushing. If shit changes and I decide to fuck her, I'll make sure you're the first to know."

His face hardens, and I can see the second we go from conversation mode to lecture mode. "Don't even think of going there," he warns.

"I'm not," I grind out. "You're the one suggesting—"

The lines around his mouth tighten. "If I have to kick your ass because you—"

I bark out a laugh. "Go home to your woman. Meiying's made it her mission to get under my skin. All I'm doing is returning the favor. Stop reading into nothing. We're good."

He doesn't look entirely convinced, but finally nods. "Fine. You going back to Kappa Eagle?"

I should, but if I go back now, it'll give Rafael the wrong idea. "Nah. I'm heading home. Gotta shift and shit. I'll catch you later."

"Later, cabrón."

I flip off my best friend as I climb into my Escalade, put it in reverse, and head for home. I pass by the sorority house and tighten my grip on the wheel until I make it to my street, three short blocks from where Meiying is living now.

Fuck. I need to get my head on straight. I'm not commitment material, and there are too many obstacles in the way, so why is it that the idea of getting past them all makes my dick twitch and brings a smile to my face?

# Chaper Five

## Meiying

"**M**om, I have to go."

"Oh, and did I tell you about the time when I was your age and—" She rattles on as though she doesn't hear me.

"Mom," I try again, shifting my bag to my other arm to avoid dropping my phone. "I'm late for class. I'll call you later. Okay?"

"Oh. Just one more thing—"

I grind my teeth together. "Mom!"

"Oh, alright. But before you hang up, can you at least tell me if you're making friends? I worry about you, sweetie." Obviously not enough since you decided to move halfway across the country to join a new Pack for a man you barely know.

I sigh. She means well and at least she's checking up on me. "Lots of friends. All the friends. Have to go now. Love you. Bye."

"Love yo—"

I hang up and all but run to my last class of the day, my sneakers squeaking as I race down the hallway, not bothering to use an ounce of my shifter stealth in my haste. My phone buzzes in my hand, but I send Mom to voicemail. I've talked to her three times already, and she just left for Florida yesterday. I think she's bored. It's a long drive, and she still has probably a day and a half before she'll get there, assuming she doesn't stop to shop along the way, which she shouldn't, but probably will. Crossing Pack boundaries is always interesting, to say the least, and if she lingers in another Pack's territory for long, she'll need to formally present herself to the Pack there. Something I know she won't bother doing. Sometimes I swear she's the most forgetful shifter I know. I even had to coordinate her travel route for her and let all of the Alpha's whose land she'd be crossing over know about her trip. If I hadn't, and she was caught, she could land in a whole heap of trouble. Not that she was worried about that in the slightest.

I sigh and chance a look at the clock on my screen. *Shit.* I'm going to be late. I'm almost to the door when another figure turns the corner on my right and crashes into me.

I drop my bag and my books tumble out onto the floor. My body sways with my momentum, but my cat-like reflexes and the stranger reaching out to catch me keep me from landing face first on the linoleum. "Ow. Crap." My skin burns where he touches me, but he doesn't let go and a snarl works its way up my throat.

"Watch where you're going," the guy snaps.

*Asshole.* I tear my arm free and ignore him, not bothering to look up as I catch sight of the silver rings decorating his hand. Urgh. What the hell?

I drop to the floor to grab my things, conscious of the time as I rush to put everything back in my bag. I'm so screwed. It's only the second day of school and I'm going to be late to my English class for the second day in a row. My skin prickles, a burning sensation licking beneath my skin as my body fights to heal the silver poisoning. The contact was brief, but that's all it takes for me to have a reaction. Dammit. That's going to annoy me for at least the next few hours before the Lyc-V in my system repairs the damage. Stupid silver. Who wears silver rings these days, anyway?

His feet edge closer, and my hackles rise. Black Beast Mode sneakers come into my line of vision, making me think of the red ones Desmond wears. *Urgh, an⟨ now I'm thinking about Desmon⟨.*

The guy crouches down and retrieves my last book before handing it to me. "Sorry. I didn't mean to snap at you. You just came out of nowhere. I'm late to my English class and my professor is known to be a real hardass. I didn't mean to take you out like that."

I accept the book, making sure my hand doesn't come into contact with his as I rise to my feet. I finally look up at the stranger beside me and honey-colored eyes framed with dark brows meet mine. I suck in a breath, my heart skipping a beat. I'm taken aback by my response to him, but the longer I stare makes me realize I'm not that surprised.

He's gorgeous in a devastating way. Medium brown skin, full lips. I wouldn't say he's light skinned, but he's not as dark as Desmond. He's wearing slim-fitting jeans that are torn in the knees and a long white crew shirt that molds to his body. Add to that the black sneakers and a black ball cap turned backwards and he's stunning in a brooding yet casual sort of way. I'm not sure how else to describe him.

Most of the skin I can see on him is covered in ink. Two forearm sleeves disappear beneath the long sleeves of his shirt that he's pushed up to his elbows, and he has a series of runes on the left side of his neck. A scroll design filled with Latin script on his right. These aren't your run-of-the-mill tattoos. I can sense the magic thrumming beneath his skin.

But despite looking like Kelly Oubre Jr's doppelganger, there's something about the way he's studying me that sets me on edge. He's not a shifter. Not a vampire. And definitely not human. What is he?

"It's fine. Sorry for slamming into you," I say, not wanting to cause issues with another faction.

The corners of his mouth curl into a calculated smirk. He licks his lips and rubs his palms together, almost like a prayer. "Nothing to be sorry about." His eyes roam over me, sliding down from my face, lingering on my chest, and then returning to my face again.

"Alrighty then." I move to step around him, but he mirrors my steps, effectively blocking me.

What is he doing?

"You have Fisks for English, right? I saw you in the back the other day." His eyes rake me over in appreciation once again. He's not even trying to hide his interest.

Normally, I'd be flattered, but right now I just want to get to class so I'm leaning toward being annoyed.

"Um. Yeah." I tuck a piece of hair behind my ear and try to ignore the way my stomach clenches. "So you know, gotta run."

I try to go around him again but his hand shoots out, gripping my forearm, and the sting of silver has me gritting my teeth as a snarl slips past my lips.

"Hold up," his voice pitches low and his eyes lock onto mine.

Mine widen in pain, a flash of trepidation slamming into me before I shove it aside and force myself to hold still, refusing to let this asshole see my pain. I don't know who this guy thinks he is, but he can't just grab me. I tug on my arm, but unlike the first time, he doesn't release me. His fingers flex, his grip tightening as his penetrating stare bores into me. The scent of burning flesh reaches my nostrils and something dark and dangerous seeps into my expression as tension bleeds into the air.

My gaze darts around us, taking in the empty hallway. Classes started almost five minutes ago, so it's just the two of us in the halls. Good. No witnesses for when I lay this guy out for daring to touch me.

He must pick up on my anger because all of a sudden he smiles, offering me an easy carefree grin. "Safety in numbers, right? Come on." Not giving me a chance to respond he gives me a conspiratorial wink and pulls me the rest of the way to our class, his hand still wrapped around me though it's slipped down, his fingers encircling my wrist.

The door to our class is already closed, but he quietly inches it open and peers inside as I tug my hand free yet again. He turns to scowl at me as I rub the ache from my wrist.

"How's it look?" I ask, trying to dispel some of the tension still thick between us. My tigress wants to strike out at him, but I know now isn't the time. I attempt to peer over his shoulder, but he's nearly a foot taller than me so I can't see much.

He gives me another smile, this one wider and seemingly more genuine, and I realize he's young. Probably a freshman like me since we're in the same English class. He still has some softness to his face, though that looks like the only place you would find any. His shoulders are broad, his waist narrow and his arms are corded with muscle. Between the body, the arrogance, and the rune tattoos, I'm betting he's a fae or a druid. I wonder if he plays Infernum. He certainly has the physique for it.

"Come on," he whispers, tugging me through the door though thankfully this time with his other hand, the one not sporting silver rings. He adjusts his hold again, capturing my hand with his, and I stare at our laced fingers with a frown, but allow him to lead me inside so as not to disturb the class.

Fisks is at the whiteboard, his back to us as he writes today's assignment on the board. He's human, so if we're quick and silent, we shouldn't draw his attention. We get a few interested looks from other students as we make our way to the empty seats in the back, my hand still locked in his as he raises his finger to his lips, the universal sign to be quiet. A few students nod and grin before turning their attention back to the front of the class.

Once safely in our seats, he releases me and I expel a relieved breath right as our professor turns around to face the class. His gaze lands on me and he frowns but doesn't comment, continuing with his lecture.

"That was a close one," the guy who crashed into me says.

I bite my bottom lip and nod. Pulling out my notebook so I can take notes on today's lecture, I do my best to block out our strange encounter, hoping that's the end of it and that he doesn't touch me again. That shit still hurts.

"I'm Deacon," he whispers, eyes straight ahead as though paying attention to Mr. Fisks.

I don't bother to respond. But after a minute passes, he asks, "What's your name?"

I consider refusing to answer, but what would be the point? It wouldn't be hard to figure out if he really wanted to.

"Meiying," I whisper under my breath.

"Nice to—"

"Mr. Hunt."

Deacon tilts his head to our professor, adopting a bored expression. "Yeah?"

"Is there something you'd like to share with the class?" Mr. Fisks asks, and there's a warning in his voice.

"Nah, I'm good," Deacon answers, unconcerned.

"Then I suggest you pay attention to today's lesson. We'll have an exam this Friday." He turns away, droning on about what will be covered on the exam and this week's assigned reading, but I'm not really paying attention. I glance at Deacon through my peripheral, only to catch his eyes on mine.

He reaches into his backpack and retrieves a notebook of his own. It's leather bound with a gnarled tree decorating the front. His large dark hands make it impossible for me to see what he's writing but I know it's not anything class related. I give myself a moment to look at his tattoos again as my curiosity gets the better of me. The marks are near black, unlike any mortal tattoos I've seen.

He tugs on the page, tearing it out before neatly folding it in half and sliding it onto my desk with an arrogant smirk.

I purse my lips and give him a questioning look. One he returns with a wink. Rolling my eyes, I reach for the note and carefully unfold it so as not to draw Mr. Fisk's attention again.

A laugh bubbles up in my throat and I cover it with a cough when I see what the note says.

He wrote, **Will you go out with me?** on the page in tight neat letters, much neater than I would have expected from a guy, with three check boxes beneath the question labeled, **Yes. No.** And **Maybe.**

My shoulders shake as I struggle to contain a snicker, my tiger finding him amusing. This guy, is he for real? What are we, five?

I reach for my pen and check the *No* box before adding a thank you beside it and discreetly passing it back to him.

He opens the note and scowls, his expression a split between genuine surprise and confusion, before he writes something else, his strokes almost aggressive before he folds the paper in half and passes it back again.

**Why not?**

I chew on my bottom lip. Because you manhandled me and burned me with silver. Because there is something about you that screams danger. And even if none of those things were true, he's not Pack, which means he can't be trusted. I have nothing against the other factions, but I'm not a moron either. Humans are safe because they're weak, but mixing with whatever he is sounds like a disaster waiting to happen. He should wear a warning sign. *Dangerous. Proceed with Caution.*

On top of all that, he's most likely a total player. I'm not really into guys who just want to take a walk on the wild side and see what being with a shifter is all about. Newsflash, it's dangerous. I'm a tiger, and despite whatever the hell he is, I doubt he can handle my beast if she decides to come out and play.

Though somehow writing any of that down seems like a bad idea, so instead I write, **I don't know you. What if you're a crazy stalker?**

I pass the note back to him and he makes quick work of his response.

**No stalker tendencies present. I'm a nice guy. Promise.** I give him a dubious look and he raises his little finger in the universal gesture for a pinkie swear.

"I'm not sure I believe you," I whisper while making sure our teacher isn't looking my way.

His brows pull together. "That I'm a nice guy or that I'm not a stalker?"

I shrug. I mean, really, it could go either way.

He huffs out a breath and snatches the paper off my desk, writing furiously before handing it back, but instead of slipping it on my desk he holds it out between us, his entire attention on me as he waits for me to take it.

A few of our classmates are giving us interested looks, but I ignore them and focus on the boy beside me. He raises his brows and waves the paper in his hand.

Urgh, fine. I hold my hand out and he slowly places it in the palm of my hand, his fingers trailing across my skin before he withdraws. I shiver.

**Give me a chance. I can see I made a shitty first impression. Let me fix that. One date.**

I fight back an eye roll before scribbling across the paper and handing it back.

**What sort of date?** I ask.

The corner of his mouth quirks. **Pizza and a movie at my place?** he answers.

Pass. I just met the guy and he expects me to go back to his place with him on a first date? Do I have booty call stamped on my forehead somewhere or something?

**Netflix and chill? Not really my thing.** I write and toss the note back to him. We're running out of space to write, so hopefully this will end soon because his date suggestion only confirms that he is a total player who wants an easy lay. *Sorry, bu••y. That isn't me.* Then again, what did I expect? Shifters are known for sharing skin privileges pretty regularly. He probably thinks I'm easy for that reason alone.

The note lands on my desk again. **Not what I meant. I figured we could do something low key. Get to know each other. Talk.** When he puts it like that, it doesn't sound *so ba•,* but it's still a bad idea and I'm not naive enough to fall for it. Or dumb enough to put myself at risk. What if he belongs to a shifter hating faction and needs a feline sacrifice? No thanks.

Desmond's face flashes through my mind. His lips pressed into a disapproving frown, a silent warning that I better fucking not. My stomach flip-flops, which only serves to annoy me more. I shake the image of him from my head. *What the hell is wrong with me? I shoul•n't care whether or not Desmon♦ woul♦ approve. Actually, I ♦on't care. Not one bit.* My tiger stretches within me in agreement. This is just a side effect of sleep deprivation and being away from Clan Cat. I barely slept last night. I'm used to my solitude, to things being quiet, but whoever is in the room over mine decided to have company over, and let's just say they stayed up into the wee morning hours doing some extracurricular activities, and had zero problem letting the entire house know about it. Even without my enhanced shifter hearing, I still would have heard all their thumbs thumps and moans.

I give Deacon another look through my peripheral. He gives me a small smile and a tilt of his head as if to say "*please?*"

**I'm not really looking to get into a relationship.** I write, and return the paper to him, somewhat frustrated at my unwillingness to give the guy a shot. I know Desmond is factoring into that decision. Even if he isn't the only reason, and I hate it. Hate that he has this invisible pull over me when I know nothing will ever happen between us, and that's a good thing. We can hardly stand one another. And even more, he's a stupid wolf. Why my tigress is interested in him at all is baffling.

Deacon's mouth dips down as he writes out his response.

**Not asking for your hand in marriage or to be your boyfriend. Just a chance to get to know you. Maybe be friends? Isn't that the entire point to Hellbound U? To mix and mingle?**

He has a point. And friends wouldn't be a horrible idea, but ... I mentally shake myself. I might regret this, but I refuse to let Desmond's imaginary disapproval decide for me. **Okay. Friends.**

His smile grows when he sees my answer. **Any suggestions for our first friend date?**

**Not a date. But how about coffee?**

**Got it. What's your number?**

We exchange phone numbers and I discreetly enter his into my phone, praying this isn't a mistake when the teacher draws everyone's attention.

"That'll be all for today. Finish your reading for the week and do not forget about Friday's exam. This will count for twenty percent of your grade, so it would behoove you not to slack off. It will be difficult to catch up should you fail and there will not be any retakes so don't think emailing me you're sick the night before will buy you any extra time to study. It won't."

A collective groan rolls through the class as everyone shuffles to their feet. "So," Deacon rubs the back of his neck. "What class do you have next?"

"Physical Combat," I tell him as we both walk out the door. His hand brushes against mine and I instinctively bring it to my chest. He doesn't notice my reaction.

"Cool. I'll walk with you. I'm going the same way."

"Sure." I mean, it is a free country. I can't very well tell him no.

We spend the next ten minutes talking about nothing and everything, and my initial apprehension begins to wane. Deacon is … charismatic. He's animated when he talks, using his hands, and his face is so expressive. He's one hundred percent as arrogant as I initially pegged him to be but, I don't know, he's not an asshole about it, despite what happened in the hallway, and he doesn't grab me again. He's fae. An Unseelie from the Shadow Court. Whatever that means. But it explains his runes and the slight point of his ears. Something I originally missed beneath the edge of his ball cap. I guess he doesn't like to advertise his faction, something I can relate to.

I find myself laughing more than I'm used to after meeting someone new. There's just something about talking to him that is, I don't know, easy. He reminds me a lot of Jordy in that way.

I discover Deacon is in fact on the Infernum team. No surprise there. He's second string seeing as he's an incoming freshman, and he's a Reaper which means he's gunning for Desmond's spot. Good for him.

He's confident and definitely a little cocky that he'll get it by the end of the year, but I know that won't happen. Not before Des graduates, at least, so Deacon will have to wait until his junior year to start.

A part of me wonders if the two of them are friends, or friendly at least, since Desmond would be the one responsible for working with him. None of the guys are particularly social unless they have to be, Desmond less so than even Rafael, and that's saying something.

In high school, the guys actively avoided everyone not in their close-knit circle, which genuinely meant anyone not Pack and definitely anyone who wasn't a part of Clan Wolf.

I can't imagine things are any different here. It's unlikely Desmond would bother getting to know an Infernum player off the field, but during training and practices, he might be less of an asshole. Maybe. Okay, probably not, but a part of me is tempted to ask Deacon how well he knows Desmond. I try not to dwell on why I want to know that, though.

We reach the school's athletic center and I turn to wave goodbye.

"See you around, Deacon," I tell him, but before I can move for the doors, he clasps my hand with his and tugs just enough to stop me.

"Okay, can you not do that?" I ask.

He drops my hand immediately, lifting his own in a show of surrender. "My bad. I just ..."

"I'm a shifter." I tell him and his brows furrow together.

"Yeah. I picked up on that."

"Okay then you know your rings hurt like a bitch every time you touch me and what, you just don't care?"

His eyes widen in surprise and he looks down at his hands. "What?"

"They're silver."

He nods. "Yeah. Silver holds magic better than most metals, it—"

"Poisons shifters. See." I hold my arm out, showing him the black spots dotting my forearm and wrist.

He curses. "I'm sorry. I didn't mean to hurt you."

I shrug, the beast in me satisfied in the knowledge that it wasn't intentional. "It's fine just, if you're wearing those," I indicate the rings on his hands, "don't touch me, okay?"

He nods, adopting a sheepish expression. "I won't."

Good. With that settled I turn to leave, but his voice stops me. "I'm glad we ran into each other today. Literally and figuratively." A slow smile spreads across his face. "You're not like other girls, Meiying. It's refreshing."

*Oh.*

"Thanks. I, uh, I'm glad we ran into each other too."

"Yeah?" he asks.

I roll my eyes. "Yeah. You're not that bad, but don't let it go to your head. I've only agreed to coffee," I remind him, and the next thing I know, he closes the distance between us, reclaiming my hand with his ringless hand as he brings it to his mouth, gently pressing his lips to my knuckles.

His eyes flick up, holding my gaze, and a small smile plays on his lips before he straightens and takes a step back. "See you around, *frien*."

"Yep." I turn and make a beeline for the doors, not sure what to think of that, when for the second time today I crash into another warm body, this time hard enough that I stumble back a few steps and only my cat-like reflexes keep me from falling. That is, until a certain asshole reaches out to steady me. His familiar scent wraps around me, catching me off guard and I mentally freak out, jerk away, and crash to the ground, landing on my butt anyways.

"Seriously!"

A warm chuckle has me looking up to find Desmond's amused stare locked on me. Not who I wanted to run into right now.

# Chaper Six

## Meiying

"I thought cats were supposed to land on their feet?" he said, peering down at me like the brooding asshole I know him to be. My fingers curl into fists against the unforgiving ground and open my mouth to snap at him for being a jerk and letting me fall, because I know he did it on purpose. Desmond's reflexes are lightning fast, thanks to his wolf, so there is zero doubt in my mind he could have caught me if he'd wanted to. But before I snap at him, his gaze shifts past me to the doors, a frown marring his face and a flash of anger ignites in his eyes. His wolf damn near glowing in his gaze.

I turn, but no one is there. I wonder briefly if he saw me talking to Deacon. And if he did, does he care? Probably not. But then where is the anger coming from? And it's anger alright. The scent of his furry rolls off him, heady and thick in the air.

I shove myself to my feet, dusting my hands on the back of my jeans. "Ha Ha. Aren't you hilarious," I deadpan.

His attention turns back to me. "Why were you walking with Hunt?" he asks, his gaze probing, like he'll find the answer in my expression alone.

"Who?"

"Hunt?" At my blank look he huffs. "Deacon Hunt. The fae you were talking to on your way over here. Why were you talking to him?"

"Am I not supposed to?" I ask, not bothering to answer his question as I head to my next class. I have ten minutes before it starts, but I'd rather Desmond think I don't have time to talk at the moment. No sense in stroking his ego by pretending I give a damn about what he has to say.

Instead of dropping it, though, he falls into step beside me, his long strides eating the distance and instinctively making me speed up until I realize what I'm doing and force myself to slow down. I am not prey. I don't run from anyone, and certainly not Desmond. I take a deep breath through my nose and try to release the tension in my body, but it does absolutely nothing for me when he's standing so close and smelling like … well, him. Urgh. My tiger wants to rub up against him and wrap herself in his scent and it's doing things to my head I definitely don't like. Why does my beast have to be such a hussy?

"He's on the team," he says, and his frown deepens. He slows down once he sees I'm no longer beside him.

"Why is that a problem? You, Rafael, and Jordy are all on the Infernum team too."

We walk in silence together for several minutes before he finally says, "It's not the same."

I bark out a laugh. "I'm sorry. How exactly is it different? Do you have a problem because he's fae?"

He glowers down at me, but I refuse to be affected.

"You know what they're like. The fae folk will fuck anything that walks. He's a player and the fact you're Pack isn't going to deter him."

I roll my eyes. "So what. Let him try." I leave out the fact he already did because I made it clear only friendship was on the table. But seeing Desmond bothered by the idea of anything happening between me and Deacon makes my beast surprisingly happy. "And shifters are any better? Don't tell me you're a prude, Des?" I joke. "It's not like you're shy about sharing skin privileges." At least not if the rumors can be trusted. And why does that bother me? I've never actually seen Desmond hook up with anyone or look like he's going to. Not at gatherings or parties. He always arrives alone and leaves the same way, keeping to himself and those of Clan Wolf, but I hear the way the other females in the Pack talk about him. And I know my brother and how frequently a new woman visits his bed. Shifter guys, especially when they're young and in their prime like Desmond is now, are absolute man sluts taking full advantage of the tactile nature of their beasts and leaning into their animal instincts to fuck anyone that catches their eye. They're definitely in no position to judge a fae for getting around when they do the same thing. Not that I'm judging, really. I know our beasts heighten our needs. I've just never wanted to get around, and despite my tiger being a hussy, she seems to only be a hussy for one particular asshole.

A growl rumbles deep in his chest and catches my tigress's attention.

She immediately perks up. "I don't share them with just anyone."

The admission brings a smile to my face.

"Right—" I draw the word out, not really sure how else to respond. "Are you struggling now that two of your besties have settled down? Must be hard to catch the ladies without your wingmen by your side these days."

Desmond's gaze sharpens. "I'm not a man-whore and I don't need a wingman to catch a girl's attention."

No. I'm sure he doesn't. "Whatever you say."

His teeth grind together. I shouldn't like upsetting him as much as I do. He's our Pack Hunter. If anything, I should respect him. But hell, all I want is to go to war with him.

"I don't have to explain myself to you."

"Ding. Ding. Ding. You are one hundred percent right."

His eyes widen the smallest amount, but it's enough to relay his surprise at my words. Oh, he made this too easy and doesn't even realize it yet.

"And I should respect that. So, I will. Your business is your business. But since you brought it up, let me remind you that I don't need to explain myself to you, either." I grin, my smile widening the darker and more hooded his expression gets.

I know Mom always said you should never poke a bear—or in this case, a wolf—but I don't think she realized just how much fun it could be.

A snarl curls the corners of his mouth.

"Stay away from him."

I shrug my shoulders. "I'll consider it."

"You will?"

I snort. "No."

He growls deep in the back of his throat. "I'm only looking out for you."

I roll my eyes. "Why? I don't need you to. I'm not some fragile human, Desmond. I'm a tiger. One little fae isn't going to hurt me let alone woo me to his bed after having just met." I've already decided I'm not dating the guy, so it's a non-issue. Not that I'll tell him that.

Desmond goes quiet again before he barks out a mocking laugh. Shaking his head, his mouth curls into a cruel smile, the one he seems to wear more and more whenever I'm around. "I shouldn't be surprised."

I frown. "Surprised by what?" I ask and then kick myself for being so damn predictable. The smart move would have been to ignore his comment. Not to play right into his hands.

His eyes burn with thinly veiled hostility. "That you've become like every other chick on campus. Both stupid and shallow. Guess you're turning into an Infernum groupie like the rest of them."

He shakes his head as though I've somehow disappointed him. "I thought you were better than that." He shrugs. "Guess I was wrong if you're already sniffing around the players."

I ignore the sharp stab of his words, but then he decides to cut a little deeper. "I give you a week, maybe two, before he gets bored." His gaze rakes over me, but there isn't a hint of desire in his eyes as they travel over my body. Instead, they hold pity and an edge of disgust. "On second thought, just the one. He'll lose interest before you hit day seven."

My cheeks heat and I know he can see the blush climbing up my neck.

"Fuck you." My voice shakes as I clench my hands into tight fists at my side. Why did that hurt so much?

He grunts. "Pass."

Fury spikes through my bloodstream, my anger and humiliation at his words filling me like a vicious, violent wave. I don't even realize what's happening until it's done. One second I'm about to storm off and the next, my fist is flying, connecting with his jaw, but only enough to graze it because dammit, he's too fucking tall.

The next thing I know Desmond is shoving me into an empty classroom. The door closes behind us and he locks it before pressing me back into the nearest wall. I suck in a breath and Desmond lifts both arms on either side of me, caging me in with his bulk. "That was an incredibly stupid thing to do." I don't miss the threat in his voice, but I absolutely choose to ignore it.

I fist both hands in the fabric of his shirt and shove him with all of my strength, but it's like trying to move a mountain. He shifts back a step before pressing back forward, drawing on his own shifter strength to keep himself in place. "I always knew you were a jerk. But I never knew you to be this cruel."

"It can't be considered cruelty if it's the truth."

Tears sting the backs of my eyes before I blink them away. *"Never let them see you cry, sweetheart,"* Mom used to tell me. When Dad left her and filed for divorce, it was the lowest I'd ever seen her, but she never did let him see her cry. She was strong. And she raised me to be strong too. I refuse to break down and cry in front of Desmond all because what, he hurt my feelings? Fuck that. His opinion means nothing to me.

"Well, thanks for clearing that up." My lower lip trembles until I sink my teeth into it, using the pain as an anchor.

Desmond is silent as he stares down his nose at me, eyes devoid of emotion.

"I fucking hate you," I tell him.

Zero reaction.

"You said your piece. Told me I'm stupid and shallow and can't hold a guy's attention. Is there anything else you need to get off your chest? I have a class to get to, and this right here," I wave my arm between us, "is a waste of my time."

His gaze latches onto my arm.

With surprising speed and gentle hands he lifts my arm up, bringing it closer to his face like he's looking for—

I mutter out a curse seeing what caught his attention. Dark smudges dot my skin where the silver of Deacon's rings came into contact with it. Shit.

Desmond's expression goes from blank to murderous as he grinds out his next words. "Who hurt you?" His already dark brown eyes turn even darker, sending a shiver down my spine.

I don't answer him.

"I'm not going to ask again, Meiying. Who. Fucking. Hurt. You?"

# Chaper Seven

## Desmond

My nostrils flare, taking in the dark signs of silver poisoning dotting Meiying's fair skin. There's no mistaking what it is. They're dark as tar with a green undertone unique to poison, and no way did she come into contact with silver by accident. Someone hurt her.

Whoever he is, he's a dead man.

Meiying's already pale skin has gone two shades paler, making her bright eyes damn near glow. Her mouth parts, tongue peeking out to lick her full bottom lip. My dick twitches and I silently curse, willing it to stand the fuck down.

She swallows hard, and I know her mind is racing for a response.

"Don't even think about lying to me," I warn.

In a move I never would have expected from her, Meiying twists her arm out of my grasp and dips beneath the arm I have pressed against the wall caging her in, in a bid for escape. It takes two seconds for her hand to reach the door, but before she can open it, I catch her by the waist and tug her back against me. "Not so fast, kitten."

Her anger and hatred for me roll off her in waves and the bitter scent of her emotions fills the air. She digs her short nails into my arms and kicks back her legs, cursing my name.

I flip her around and press her against the door, using my body to pin her in place. I've tried to keep myself in check, but she is not making this shit easy and my wolf is demanding, urging me to make her submit. Why does she always have to challenge me like this? I'm not like other wolves. I'm hunter-born, so I shouldn't need to assert my dominance over her, but I do. It's driving me insane, making the beast in me ride my human half harder than ever before.

"Get off of me," she shouts, and I cover her mouth with my palm, my hand so large I damn near cover half her face. Fuck she's small. Fragile. I know she isn't human. Isn't weak like some of the others who roam these halls, but the difference in our size makes my protective instincts spring forward.

Her eyes blaze and I lean in, ensuring she sees that I am not fucking around right now. Not when it comes to something like this.

"Don't you dare open that pretty little mouth of yours and scream like that again. Do you feel me? Unless you're ready to tell me who the fuck was dumb enough to hurt you, or decide to drop down on your knees and wrap your lips around my cock, your mouth is going to stay closed."

Her eyes narrow, nostrils flaring as her tiger glares at me through her gaze. She's so fucking pissed, and I wish I had more time to enjoy it. I've worked hard this past year getting Meiying to hate me. It makes keeping her out of my bed a hell of a lot easier that way. But damn if seeing her like this doesn't make my dick hard, and the thought of her on her knees for me … fuck. I can't be the only one affected by that image.

Her small fingers wrap around my wrist, pulling to get my hand off of her mouth.

"Are you going to behave?"

If looks could kill I'd be dead right now with the way she's glaring at me.

"It's a yes or no question, kitten. Blink twice for yes. Once for no."

Her eyes narrow to slits. Seconds pass and the air grows impossibly thick. I'm sure she can feel my hard-on pressed against her stomach, but neither of us is going to acknowledge it. I catch a hint of arousal in her scent, throwing me off when she finally blinks twice and concedes. A rush of satisfaction swells inside my chest. I drop my hand, but don't step away. I rationalize that the moment I do she'll bolt. It has nothing to do with how fucking good she feels with her tight little body up against mine. Her lips are pressed into a thin line, her cheeks scarlet. A mix of anger and indignation. She is so fucking beautiful like this.

A few strands of her black hair fell from her hair tie during our struggle and I slowly reach out, tucking the flyaways behind her ear. Her eyes are guarded as I trail one finger down the side of her face before cupping her jaw. She closes her eyes, a small shudder moving through her.

"What's his name, Meiying?" I ask, and there's a bite of steel in my tone.

Her eyes snap open and she bears her teeth. "You're making a big deal out of nothing. It was an accide—"

"No man leaves a mark on a female by accident." My voice is deceptively calm. I lean down closer to her until our breaths mingle. "Was it Hunt? Did he do that?" The sudden widening of her eyes gives her away, and my vision goes red.

My jaw flexes and I go to step back, but she latches onto me, wrapping her arms around my neck. "Whatever it is you're thinking of doing, don't. It was an accident. I don't think he realized his rings would hurt me." I fight the urge to encircle her waist and rise to my full height, taking her with me.

Her arms tighten as her feet lift from the ground. "Desmond—"

"His rings?" I snarl. "He touched you." I look down at her arms and wrist. Repeatedly by the looks of it. "You can't protect your boyfriend," I tell her. "Not from this."

Her feet sway off the floor and her arms tighten around my neck, squeezing to maintain her hold on me since I haven't bothered to help her out.

"He's not my boyfriend. We literally just met because I slammed into him running late to class." My pulse jumps at her words. "I don't even know the guy. We have one class together and this is the first time we've spoken."

I grab the backs of her thighs, hoisting her higher up. Her legs wrap around my waist and my hands move to her ass. I lean her back against the door and wait to see if she'll demand to be put down. She doesn't. Neither does she yell at me for the way I'm cupping her ass right now.

"If you're protecting him—"

She snorts. "I'm not. I have no reason to, so get off your high horse. I'm not some damsel in need of saving."

"Is that so?" I ask, shifting my hips so her center grinds down on my cock.

She gasps. "What are you doing?"

I repeat the movement, and she shakes in my arms. "Are you sure you're not in need of saving?"

# Chaper Eight

## Meiying

I ignore the way my heart is racing in my chest.

"By the guy who just called me stupid, shallow, and implied I was unattractive and incapable of holding a man's attention?" I shake my head. "I think I'm good."

There's a flash of something in his gaze I can't quite put my finger on. His hold tightens on my ass and his dick strains against his jeans, pressing firmly between my thighs. What was I thinking wrapping my legs around him like this?

As if hearing my thoughts, Desmond smirks. *Asshole.* I decide to give him a taste of his own medicine.

Using his shoulders for leverage, I raise myself up a few inches and roll my hips over his length in a long caress. He sucks in a breath, his eyes dark and filled with challenge. Take that, asshole.

Holding his stare, I do it again, and his entire body trembles with need. I'm not blind. Despite his earlier words, he wants me. He won't after today, and I can live with that, but right now at this very moment, Desmond Pierce wants to fuck me, and knowing that sends a flood of euphoria surging through me. This means he's no longer in control here. I'm the one with all the power now.

"Don't start something you can't finish."

"Why not? It's not like you could possibly want me, right? So why would me doing this," I grind my pussy against him again, liquid heat soaking my panties and the scent of my arousal filling the air, "matter to you? You can't possibly be affected, right?"

He doesn't say a word, but when I give another deliberate roll of my hips, he digs his fingers into my ass cheeks and thrusts upward, grinding his dick into me in response.

To my complete horror, a purr escapes me, and he levels me with a knowing smirk.

I dig my short nails into his shoulders as he dry humps me against the classroom door in long languid thrusts and Oh. My. God. That feels good.

One of his hands comes up to knead my breast and I shamelessly arch into his touch. He growls against the corner of my mouth and the sound snaps something in me, lifting some of the pleasure-induced haze from my eyes.

*Why do I let him make me feel like this? I fucking hate him.*

Taking a deep breath, I lean forward, licking and biting my way up his neck until my lips graze the shell of his ear. "What would you do if I told you to fuck me?" I whisper and swirl my tongue along his flesh, tasting the salt on his skin.

His sharp intake of breath lets me know I've surprised him and he freezes, pulling back just enough to meet my gaze. His eyes are drowning in need, his wolf staring back at me with a fierce hunger, but there's a hint of confusion too, so I decide to taunt him some more. I make a show of licking my lips and his eyes immediately drop to my mouth.

"You'd like that, wouldn't you?"

He doesn't answer, but his muscles strain against his skin, the veins in his neck protruding.

"I bet you'd like it even more if I begged for it. Got down on my knees and showed you just how bad I—"

His fist tangles in my hair and he yanks my face toward his, tilting my head so his lips can capture my own. His kiss is savage and hungry as he claims my mouth with his tongue in long greedy stokes. I moan into his mouth, and that only seems to spur the beast inside him on. I can sense the moment he gives up control and relinquishes himself to his wolf's instincts.

His grip holds me in place, leaving me no choice but to accept his punishing kiss. The hand in my hair moves to the side of my neck in a possessive hold while the other continues to hold me up, kneading my ass. He pulls away from the door and carries me further into the room, his mouth never leaving mine until I feel a solid surface beneath me.

Desmond sets me down on a long table, but he doesn't release me. "That what you want?" he asks, and it takes me a few seconds to remember what I said to him before that kiss. "You want me to fuck you while you beg for my cock?"

*God, yes.* Not that I'll ever admit it out loud. Instead, I lean back, pressing my palms on the table to hold myself up. His hand slips from my neck right as I say, "No thanks. I think I'm good." Careful to keep my voice flat and free of emotion.

I allow a smirk to curl the corners of my mouth as I raise both brows, giving him a disinterested look.

He glares at me in disbelief and then something in him shifts. Tension crackles like lightning between us, and I fight not to squirm under his intense stare. It's the stare of an Alpha, demanding me to get in line, but Desmond isn't my Alpha and despite the urge I have to bow my head, to look away and offer him my submission, that's all it is. An urge driven by instinct, but one I don't actually have to listen to.

"You almost had me," he tsks with an amused laugh. "Almost. But if you think for one second I'm going to buy that mouthful of lies, guess again, kitten." He steps into me, cupping my sex and driving the heel of his palm against me. "Your soaked pussy doesn't lie. I can smell your need and feel how wet you are through your jeans."

My eyes pop wide and my heart beats frantically against my chest before I can pull myself together enough to bite out, "Screw you."

"You'd like that, wouldn't you?" He smirks, palm still pressed firmly against my center. My hips lift off the table of their own volition when he pushes down on my clit. I gasp, biting back a moan, and my cheeks burn with humiliation, but I can't find it in me to tell him to stop. It feels so good.

"I don't like liars," he grunts, his eyes locked on his hand between my legs. *Wait. What?* He drags my hips to the edge of the table until my butt is about to slide off. Then he spreads my legs, creating enough room for him to step between them. He makes no effort to mask his desire as he slams his lips down on mine again and groans into my mouth right before he fists my hair and jerks my head back, tearing his lips from mine and leaving me to stare up at the ceiling. He scrapes his teeth along the column of my throat, nipping and sucking on my sensitive skin.

I gasp, and a fresh wave of pleasure filters through me, igniting every cell in my body.

He runs his nose up the side of my neck, inhaling me as he says, "So, I have to punish you." There's a note of regret in his voice, and the next thing I know, he's spun me around to face the opposite wall. My feet hit the floor, my body bent over the desk and my ass thrust out toward him. One hand presses down on the center of my spine, effectively pinning me in place as the other roams over my hip, trailing down to my ass.

"What am I being punished for?" My heart rate picks up. The human half of me wants to fight him off, shout at him for daring to pin me down like this, but my tiger is damn near purring. Loving this display of dominance from him.

"You lied to me."

I shake my head in denial. "I didn't lie." My voice shakes, but whether from desire or fear, I'm not entirely sure.

"There you go again," he tsks.

His hand dips lower, boldly stroking the inside of my thighs as he uses his legs to force me into a wider stance. I grind my teeth together to hold back the moan that threatens to spill past my lips.

"I'm going to give you a second chance to come clean, because despite what you think, I'm not a complete asshole."

I start to laugh, but the sound dies in my throat when I feel the ridge of his cock dig into my ass, hard and demanding. What is he doing to me? We don't get along. We definitely don't like one another. But the level of need I feel right now is like nothing I've felt before, which is both exhilarating and terrifying at the same time because this is bad. So fucking bad.

"Do you want me to fuck you, kitten?" My mouth goes dry as he thrusts against me, pressing his cock against the crack of my ass as he mimics fucking me. "Do you want to beg for my cock as I thrust deep inside you?"

My pussy clenches and his vulgar words almost undo me. I swallow hard and manage to deliver a shaky denial. "No."

He stops moving and exhales a sigh full of resignation, as if my response somehow pains him. "I did warn you," he says, his voice tinged with regret. And okay yeah, lying to a wolf is probably not my smartest move. Shifters can scent strong emotions, those who are Alpha's or hunter-born even more so than most, so he definitely scented that lie.

I swallow hard, wondering what he intends to do next. I've never seen him like this. He's always been so restrained. So in control. We fight, sure, but with words. This isn't anything like our usual battles. This is like going to war, and I am wholly outmatched and unprepared for this kind of fight.

One hand reaches around me and undoes the button on my jeans.

"Last chance," he offers, but words die on my tongue. My thighs tighten in anticipation. Is he...are we going to...

His fingers hook into my jeans, dragging them over my hips and exposing my rear. He leaves my underwear in place, but all I'm wearing is a hot pink thong that leaves my entire backside on display. "Fuck," he groans and cups my ass cheeks, spreading them with his fingers while also pushing me forward, father across the table until the tops of my thighs can't go any further.

"Tell me to stop," he growls. "If you're not okay with this, whatever the fuck is about to happen right now, tell me now." He runs his fingers down the crack of my ass until he reaches my pussy and presses his fingers into me through the soaked fabric of my panties. My legs quake.

I should do what he suggests, tell him to stop, but I'm drunk on desire, feeling like I'll explode if he stops touching me, so I keep my lips pressed together and shake my head. I'll regret this come morning.

I won't be able to pretend this didn't happen. I won't be able to forget his hands on me or the sensation of him thrusting between my thighs. This is a mistake and I know it. I just don't fucking care.

Desmond twists his hand in my hair and I instinctively know what comes next. It's no surprise when he yanks on it, forcing my back to arch and my chin to jut forward. He seems to like that, pulling my hair. And I can't say that I'm complaining about it.

I don't have a lot of experience in this arena. I've fooled around before, sure. Given head. Had my pussy eaten out. But I haven't gone all the way with anyone. I'm not saving myself for marriage or anything like that, I just never cared about any of my past boyfriends enough to spread my legs for them. My tiger didn't purr for them. Didn't want to be marked by them. The way she does for him.

I've never been with a guy like this. One who my being responds to on a visceral level.

Des shifts to the side, no longer between my thighs, but he doesn't let go of my hair. He winds it around his fist, tightening his hold as his other hand hooks beneath the fabric of my panties and a lone finger slips between my wet slit.

I moan when he finds my clit, brushing his finger over the sensitive nub.

"Desmond ..." I gasp, and his finger moves faster against me, my hips rearing back of their own accord. The pain in my scalp and the pleasure between my thighs has pure heat zipping down my spine. My toes curl and I'm panting heavy, my release so incredibly close.

"Don't say I didn't warn you," he mutters under his breath right before he withdraws his finger from between my legs and his palm slaps my bare ass cheek. I yelp, jolting forward, but the table makes it impossible to go anywhere.

*Holy fuck.* "Did you just spank me?"

Instead of answering, he spanks my other cheek and I slap my palm against the table, a snarl pouring from my throat.

"I warned you what would happen if you didn't tell the truth." He massages my burning flesh, lessening the sting a bit, only to slap me again. I cry out, but the sound is cut off when he releases my hair only to wrap his hand over my mouth.

"Shhhh...." he whispers. "Keep making that sound and someone is bound to come and investigate what is going on in here."

I try to shift away from him. When he said he was going to punish me for lying, I didn't expect this.

He chuckles, like my attempt at escape amuses him. "I'm not done with you yet. I think you deserve at least two more." A fourth smack is delivered and I scream, but his palm muffles the sound.

"Your ass turns the prettiest shade of pink," he tells me, and I whimper against his palm.

He squeezes my ass, trailing his fingers over each cheek and between my cleft. He said two more, but he's only delivered one, and the anticipation of what is still to come grips my chest.

Desmond lets go of my mouth and shifts behind me, pressing his erection against me. "Want to try again?" he asks, rocking his hips against me. "Tell me the truth and maybe I'll consider giving you what you want. Beg for my cock the way we both know you want to."

The smug sound of his voice has my eyes narrowing and I lift my head to look over my shoulder. I won't beg for anything. Not from him or anyone else. My gaze collides with his, and just as I open my mouth to tell him to fuck off, his palm slaps my ass, harder than all of the times before.

I open my mouth on a silent scream before sucking in a shaky breath as I sag against the table.

Desmond steps back, moving around the table until he's standing in front of me, able to meet my gaze. He casually leans forward, pushing the hair out of my face. I should stand up. At the very least pull my jeans back over my ass, but I can't seem to find the energy to move.

"You know, you're not nearly as insufferable when you're like this."

I raise one hand and flip him off.

He laughs and then, unsurprisingly, walks out of the classroom without so much as a goodbye.

# Chaper Nine

## Desmond

I left Meiying bare-assed in that classroom. Zheng's little sister. Ass cheeks red, courtesy of yours truly, and on display for anyone who walked in to see. This is bad. Already, there is a voice in my head that whispers, *you traitor, he's like a brother. He trusts you. All while my wolf is urging me to turn around, to go back to that classroom and claim what is mine.*

There's a lead weight in my gut. I shouldn't have touched her. I sure as shit shouldn't still be thinking about touching her. Marking her. Owning her body and soul.

Thank God I didn't go through with fucking her. Not that what I did constitutes as much better. A heavy blanket of guilt encompasses me. This can't happen again. Me. Her. I lied when I told Rafael I wasn't interested. What I meant was I can't afford to be interested. Not in her. Not like that.

I reach the locker room and make quick work of changing. I'm a few minutes late for practice, but no one will care. My jaw tightens when I think about Deacon Hunt. He's going to get a piece of my mind when I lay his ass out on the field.

Meiying might say it was an accident, but I'm not buying it. The fucker knows what silver does to our kind. Wearing it, grabbing her, that shit is intentional.

Seeing those marks on her arm ... I shake my head and take a deep breath. It damn near sent me over the edge. The thought of anyone hurting her, anyone who isn't me—and yeah, I realize how fucked up that is—makes my blood boil.

I want to fuck her. Punish her. Soothe her. I want her to ache because of me and I want to be the only one capable of taking that ache away.

Smacking her ass and watching it redden has blood rushing straight to my cock. Seeing her lust-drenched eyes, feeling just how soaking wet her panties are, *shit,* it does something to me. And those flashes of her beast, when her tigress caught me in her gaze and called to my wolf ... I curl my hands into fists. Why do I respond to her in such a visceral way?

The door leading to the field opens and Jordy walks in, shouting, "Yeah, yeah. I'll be back. Chill the fuck out," over his shoulder.

"It's about time you showed up. Everything good?" he asks, seeing me on the bench.

I grunt. "Peachy."

He opens his locker, the one right next to mine, and gives me a curious look.

"What'd you do?" he asks.

"What are you talking about?"

He grabs a roll of athletic tape and begins wrapping his wrists. "You look guilty as fuck, man. Where were you before you got here?"

I keep my expression blank. "I think you've been watching too many *telenovelas* with Joaninha, J."

He chuckles. "You got me there, but bro, Señora Acero is savage. That opening scene is *a la Game of Thrones* two-thousand thirteen. A wedding. A massacre. Wolves tearing the enemy apart. You don't know what you're missing."

"I'll take your word for it."

He finishes with his wrists and tosses the tape back in his locker. "I still can't believe you stopped watching at the ten-minute mark." He shakes his head. "Fifteen more minutes and it would have gotten to the good part."

"I couldn't understand anything." The whole thing is in Spanish.

Jordy scoffs. "Turn on the fucking subtitles. It's fine."

I stretch my back and put myself through a short series of stretches as we bullshit a little longer. I know what I'm planning to do once I walk out on the field, but what I don't know is how to get Jordy and Rafael to leave me alone long enough to handle it.

"Hunt," I shout, ensuring my voice carries across the Infernum field. His head jerks up and he looks around, searching for whoever called his name. As soon as he realizes it was me, he jogs his way over.

"Yo. What's up?" He tilts his head in greeting, wiping the sweat from his brow with the back of his arm. The black runes that mark his arms stand out along his flesh, and the silver bands on his fingers glint in the sunlight, making my wolf's hackles rise.

"Meiying Liu." I bite out her name.

He smirks, a glint of excitement in his eyes. "She's *fine,* right? But she's no wolf. I wasn't sure if you knew her." He rocks back on his heels and gives me a knowing look. Like we're friends or some shit and both in on the same secret.

Until this moment, I had zero issue with Hunt. Thought he was an okay dude even for a fae. But now... I can't stand the sight of him, and I'm two seconds away from punching him in the face, making sure to leave a mark like he left on Meiying.

But I decide to give him a chance and delay punching him right out of the gate by grabbing him by the jersey instead and shoving him against the chain-link fence that surrounds the field.

He brings his arms up in a vain attempt to stop me, the runes on his skin glowing with some sort of magic I don't recognize, but I ensnare him in my wolf's gaze and give him a feral look. "You can try and defend yourself or you can take the beating that is coming your way. Either way, I'm getting my pound of flesh." Deacon is muscular, stacked like every other person on our team, but I have an easy sixty pounds of muscle on him and a pissed off wolf living beneath my skin. He's still a kid, so fae or not, he's weaker than I am and he's not getting away until I get what I came for.

"What the fuck, man." His eyes are wide and he grunts with the effort to throw me off him, but it's of little use. Electricity sparks against my skin, his magic crashing through my veins in a painful jolt through my system, but all it does is serve to piss off my wolf even more. I make sure he gets a good look at the fury riding me. At the beast inside me looking through my eyes and marking him as prey.

"Is she yours or something? Shit, man. I thought you stuck to your own kind. I never would have hit on her if I knew it would cause problems with you or any of the wolves." He stops fighting me, both arms raised in surrender. Idiot. So he wasn't just trying to hurt her. He was trying to claim her too? To take what is mine? I don't allow myself to dwell on my possessive thoughts, instead snarling into his face, "She's seventeen."

"So what? We're both freshmen. I'm only a year older, probably less than that."

I shake him before slamming him against the fence harder. I can feel the eyes of the team on me, but no one interferes. The only people dumb enough to try are Rafael and Jordy, and I made sure both were occupied in the locker room before tracking Deacon down, and that shit took some maneuvering.

"She's a fucking minor," I seethe.

"Bro, lay off. It's not illegal or anything. Shifters consider anyone under twenty-one a juvenile, so what's the issue?"

Shouting comes from the other side of the field. Fuck. I thought I'd have more time, but I guess I'll have to make do with what I have.

"Whatever you think is going on between you two, it ends now.

When you see her in class you're going to pretend like you don't even see her. She doesn't exist for you. And you won't ever fucking touch her again. Got it?"

His jaw tightens, and I know he wants to smart off, but he manages to keep his mouth shut. Only the flaring of his nostrils betrays his emotions. Maybe he isn't that stupid after all.

I drop my hold on him and turn, shouldering past the guys on the team stupid enough to have inched their way closer. Fucking gossips.

"Des—" Rafael calls out, but I shake my head. I'm good. Shit is over. Or at least it should be, but then Deacon goes and opens his fucking mouth.

"I'm not passing on her," he shouts. "If you had your shot and missed it, that's on you. But I'm not gonna look past a fine as fuck piece of ass for your benefit. Not until I've sampled her, at least. When I'm done, I might consider sharing if you still want a taste." He laughs. Fucking fae.

My head turns almost as if in slow motion. Everything around me falls away, and all I see is the dipshit in front of me, the three meters between us, and the time it will take me to reach him so I can lay his punk ass out.

"Am I right, boys?" Deacon smirks as he looks around him, meeting the eyes of our teammates. No one responds to him and I watch in satisfaction as his smile slips, and then, I'm on him. I have my left hand on his throat, the right clenched into a tight fist and I draw my arm back.

Right as I move to swing, a hand wraps around my fist, barely managing to stop my momentum. I jerk my gaze to my right only to find Rafael holding onto me. Jordy not two steps behind him.

"You'll start something," he bites out.

With my left hand still holding Deacon in place, I shake my best friend off. "I don't give a shit." And yeah, maybe I should. I don't know how important this asshole is to the fae faction. If beating his ass will cause problems and blow back on the Pack, but right now, I don't care even if it does, because it will be worth it. Only Rafael doesn't seem to agree.

"You know the rules. We can't engage in shit like this off the field. Back off, Des. Be smart."

With my eyes locked on his, I ignore Deacon's failed attempts at escape. His hands swing out in a bid to hit me first, save face in front of the team, but my reach is longer than his and all he manages to hit is air. He realizes that he'll never reach me and starts pounding his fist into my left arm, sinking his magic into my skin. It burns like a thousand fire ants biting into me. I grunt, but don't let go.

"Don't be stupid. You're better than this." Jordy says, and I can tell he's trying to stay calm. To talk me off the ledge, only I'm not hearing him.

"Fuck you," Deacon wheezes.

My arm is numb. He tagged me on my funny bone and the nerve is spasming, but I'm not about to let up. The glow of his runes is diminishing. His magic is running out.

Without looking at him, I tighten my grip on his neck.

Jordy appears on my other side and both he and Rafael work together to shove me back using the combined strength of their wolves to peel me away, but I drag Deacon backward with me.

"Dude, let go," Jordy shouts.

"No."

"God dammit," Rafael snaps. "For once, will you fucking listen? He isn't worth it."

My nostrils flare. "You have no idea what—"

Jordy curses. "Dammit, Desmond. He's turning blue. Shit. I didn't know black could turn that shade of blue."

I turn to Deacon, eyes narrowing. "Idiot. He's not turning blue. He's turning white. See, around his mouth the color is muted and almost ashy."

Jordy leans in for a closer look and I use my free hand to smack him upside the head.

"Fucker," he complains, rubbing the back of his head.

"I think you should see a doctor if you think that is blue. Are you color blind?"

Deacon is still struggling, but the strength has been leached out of him and his swings are more like pats on the arm now.

"Not fucking helping," Rafael bites out.

"Right." Jordy gives me his best impression of a serious look. "Drop him, man."

I quirk a brow. "That the best you got?"

"Drop him," Rafael repeats, leveling me with his wolf's gaze. I'll give him credit, his stare is damn near as threatening as his father's, but I'm hunter-born, so he knows that doesn't work on me. Not unless I want it to.

"What the hell are you all standing around for? Get to moving," Coach shouts, but his voice is far away, which means he hasn't caught sight of Deacon yet.

"Fuck." That was Jordy.

"*Hijo ²e puta.*" And that would be Rafael. I've heard *cabrón* out of his mouth enough times to know it basically translates to fucker or smartass, but this one is new.

"What was that?"

"Son of a bitch," Jordy supplies before adding on a groan, "We are so fucked."

I glare at Deacon, seeing the fearful panic in his eyes. I sigh and let go. He slumps to the ground, gasping for breath while clawing at his throat. Coach is about halfway across the field, so we have maybe another minute before this becomes an issue. Enough time for Deacon to get his pussy ass off the ground and fall into line.

I crouch down in front of him, balancing on the balls of my feet, and drop a heavy hand on his shoulder. He's coughing and wheezing, but still manages to look my way, letting me know he's aware of the very real threat I still pose. "You think my issue is that I'm jealous of a punk like you? I'm not. My problem with you is that you left silver poisoning on Meiying's skin, and when I told you to stay the fuck away from her, you mouthed off."

"What the fuck?" Jordy starts, but I ignore him. I reach down and grab Deacon's hand, tearing the three rings he wears from his fingers and curling my fists around the metal. It burns my hand immediately on contact and I squeeze my fist tighter, grunting at the pain until smoke rises from my hand.

I'm going to get my point across to this asshole one way or the other. Meiying is off limits, and if he ever lays a hand on her again, I'll fucking kill him. And in case he gets any ideas, I want him to know that the burn of silver isn't strong enough to stop me.

I grab his chin with a near bruising grip and force him to look up, his back arching from the ground, but he's too weak to fight me. "After today. You're going to pretend you don't know her. You won't look at her. You won't talk to her and you sure as fuck will not touch her. Do you understand?"

He gives a slight nod.

"Good." I release him and stand. "Because the next time I come for you, it won't be anywhere with witnesses."

I stalk toward the field, dropping the rings into my pocket and planning to intercept Coach, when I hear Jordy shout, "Puta maire, Que te Folle un Pez!" and turn just in time to see him slam his fist into Deacon's face while he's still on the ground. He knocks him out cold with the single hit.

"What the fuck did that mean?" I ask Rafael, a smile curling my lips.

He smirks and tilts his head to the side, thinking. "The literal translation?"

I nod.

"Motherfucker, I hope you get fucked by a fish."

I choke on a laugh. "What? Why a fish?"

He shrugs as Jordy—worked up and chest heaving like he just ran drills—joins us.

"It's harsher in Spanish," Rafael adds.

Jordy glares at us both, anger clouding his eyes. "You better start explaining what you meant about him leaving marks on Baby Liu."

Rafael's eyes narrow, a vicious glint in his eyes as he takes a step toward Deacon, who is still prone on the ground. I grab his jersey and shake my head. "Not now," I grunt, knowing exactly what he's thinking and agreeing. One hit isn't enough to satisfy any of our need for retribution, which is why he never should have gotten in my way.

His mouth tightens, but he concedes. Then, loud enough for a few of our teammates to hear he says. "Deacon Hunt hurt one of our females and is going to learn real fucking fast we won't tolerate abusive assholes on this team."

A few of the guys nod their heads, gazes sharpening with that information. Lines are being drawn in the sand as we speak, and I for one can't wait for Deacon to get his next dose of fuck-you medicine.

# Chaper Ten

## Meiying

I ignore the sounds of partying going on in other parts of the house and focus on my textbook. I've done a pretty good job of hiding from my housemates. I probably shouldn't. My mom keeps sending me messages and leaving voicemails asking if I've made any new friends yet. Kind of hard to do when you're actively avoiding everyone. It's just not the same as living in the Compound. There are no other tigers here, let alone shifters. Most of my housemates are witches, fae, or human. And despite knowing that, there's this strange irrational part of me that thinks if any of them see me, they'll know.

They'll know that three days ago Desmond Pierce dry humped me against a wall before baring my ass in an empty classroom and spanking me. And worse, they'll know I liked it.

I groan miserably into my hands. There has to be something wrong with me when that thought alone has me clenching my thighs and aching for something else to be between them. I guess at this moment it's a good thing I'm not living in the Compound, or everyone within twenty feet of me would be asking why the scent of lust clings to my skin.

My bedroom door swings open. "Meiying!" A female voice singsongs, startling me. "Why are you studying right now when you should be hanging out with me!"

Quinn skips into my room wearing a bright orange bikini top and a pair of cut-off denim shorts. She plops down on my bed beside me, an exaggerated pout on her face.

"You're drunk," I tell her. Lucky duck. Alcohol doesn't have the same effect on me given my shifter metabolism.

She rolls her eyes and lets out a huff. "Obviously. And you should be, too." Then with a whine she adds, "I'm sorry."

I frown at her over the edge of my book. "What is there to be sorry for?"

"I'm your big sister. I'm supposed to make your Kappa Eagle experience epic, and instead of having fun with us you're holed up in your room doing homework." She throws herself back on my bed dramatically. "I've failed you."

I roll my eyes. Drunk Quinn is an interesting sight to behold. "You have not failed me," I tell her. "You're a great big sister."

She perks up. "I am?"

I shrug. Why not? It's not like I have anything to compare her to, and I didn't really come here with any expectations. She's answered any questions I've had and she hasn't been a jerk like some of the other girls in the house, so I'd say we were off to a good start. Besides, I'm a cat and I like my solitude. For the most part I've been left alone. A fact I very much appreciate.

"Yep. The best." I turn back to my book, hoping that'll be that and she'll see herself to the door.

"Great. Then as your amazing big sister, I demand you party!" She cheers as she jumps from the bed with a fresh wave of energy. "We need drinks!"

"I'm supposed to study," I tell her, resisting her efforts to drag me from my bed. "And alcohol doesn't really affect me."

"You can study later. You need to have fun! We have special brews that will help you get a buzz. Come on. It'll be fun!"

"I should study. I need to pass my classes," I remind her, but she doesn't seem worried.

"You will. You're smart. So come on. There's no time like the present."

"Fine," I sigh, and let her drag me from my room. After today's nightmare of an exam that I am eighty percent sure I completely bombed, I guess I can take a short break and hang out for a little bit. Besides, it doesn't look like she's going to take no for an answer.

Quinn pulls me down the hall and through the main part of the house before pausing right as we get to the doors leading into the backyard. "Clothes!"

"Uh, what about them?"

She whirls on me. "You need them!" She makes a show of smacking her own forehead. "Come on. You need to change."

Now I'm being dragged back the way we came, but instead of going into my room where, you know, all my clothes are, she pulls me into hers and starts rifling through her closet.

"What are you doing?"

She pulls pieces out left and right, tossing them behind her on the floor after she rejects them. "You do know you're going to have to clean that up, right?" I remind her.

"The guys from Alpha Ze are here."

Yippee, stupid drunk frat boys. I am so excited. Cue the sarcasm.

"Your point?"

She turns and scowls at me, waving what looks like a purple crop top in my face. "So? So, you're wearing that?"

"What's wrong with what I'm wearing?" I ask, looking down at my jean shorts and oversized crew neck t-shirt.

"Are you modest?" she asks, ignoring my question and going back to sifting through her clothes.

I snort. "Shifters and modesty don't usually go together. Why?" Sort of hard to be modest when you have to strip naked every time you want to shift.

"Because you're always covered up. You're in college. This is where you go to see others and be seen."

I open my mouth to tell her I don't have any desire to be seen by the other students here when she waves a piece of black fabric in the air. "Found it!" She jumps up and down twice. Like she just won a carnival prize. "Okay, here. Get naked and put this on."

She tosses it to me and I catch the black, silky material. "A swimsuit?" I toss it back to her. "I don't want to go swimming." I'm a cat. I don't particularly like the water. At least not initially. It's like instinct dictates I, at the very least, curl my lip over the idea.

She throws it at me again. "You don't wear a swimsuit to go swimming, silly. You wear it so you have an excuse to walk around half naked. Now, hurry up and try it on. You can use my bathroom."

I snort, because my room, which is right next door, is so far away.

Quinn gives me her best shot at an *I'm waiting* look, and I decide to humor her. She's basically the closest thing to a friend I have here, and pissing her off probably won't do me any favors.

In the bathroom, I strip out of my clothes and hold the swimsuit out in front of me. It's a one piece, so that's good at least. I wasn't lying when I said I wasn't particularly modest, but I'm not a let it all hang out type of girl unless a shift is about to follow. There are what look to be a dozen little ties and crisscross straps, and I'm not exactly sure how to put the damn thing on.

"Are you decent?" Quinn calls, knocking on the door.

"No." I tell her, one leg in a hole I'm not entirely sure is meant for my leg.

"Too bad, I'm coming in." And she does. When she sees me, naked and jumping on one foot as I try to get my leg out of the weird knot thingy, she covers her mouth and laughs, eyes wide and shoulders shaking.

"I'm still naked!" I say, not bother to cover up, though. It's not like I have anything she hasn't seen before.

"I can see that." She's laughing so hard, her eyes are watering. "Need a little... help?" She waves at me and I huff out a breath.

"Obviously, yes. I don't know how the heck to get into this."

She giggles and moves closer, helping me untangle my foot as I try to keep myself from tipping over.

"Here, step in through this one." She helps me slip my feet into the right holes. Why are there so many? And then turns her back so I can shimmy into the thing.

The more on it goes, the less it actually covers, if you can believe that. "Okay, I'm turning back around," she calls and then helps me find the holes to slip my arms through.

She gives me a critical once over, pulling the fabric here, tightening it there, before stepping back to examine her work. "You look fucking hot!" she says, a gleam in her eye.

I look down for a second before squeezing my eyes closed. "Are you sure you didn't give me lingerie?" I ask, because, wow. And I don't mean that in a good way. Quinn grabs my shoulders and turns me to face the mirror. I open one eye and gasp.

"Holy fu—"

"I know. Right?" She grins. "This one used to be my favorite but since I got these done," she points at her chest, " it doesn't fit anymore. It looks great on you though, so you can keep it."

Keep it? I'm not sure it's even legal to wear. Not in public, at least. What I thought was a sleek black one piece is really lingerie pretending to be a swimsuit. The front has a plunging neckline that goes down past my navel, exposing the top of my crotch—thank god I got waxed last week. Holding the two sides in place is a series of crisscross ties that lace up the entire front until they reach my neck, where they tie like a halter top in the back. The material over my boobs barely covers my nipples, so I have an insane amount of cleavage, and the back is virtually nonexistent. My entire back is on display and half my ass hangs out of the teeny tiny bottoms, giving me a persistent wedgie.

"Stop adjusting everything," Quinn chides, smacking my hand away as she tugs my bottoms up, not down, exposing even more of my ass. "It's supposed to be like this."

I gawk at her. "I'm almost naked. Actually, I think this is more provocative than being naked."

Her smile is wide. "I know, right? Now let's go get wasted! It's Friday night and you've been here a week already. It's time to let loose. I promise we have stuff that works on shifters, so no excuses."

Before I can object, she is literally dragging me out of the bathroom. "Quinn. Stop."

Does she? Of course not. And who would have guessed that my five-foot-four sorority witch was this strong. We're back at the door and not giving me any time to prepare myself, she swings it wide open and shouts, "Time for Jell-O shots, bitches!"

The girls outside laugh and cheer, and then with all the confidence in the world, Quinn heads for the table where said Jell-O shots are lined up in a rainbow of colors that glitter and swirl with magic. Several of my sorority sisters move to follow her, everyone barely dressed in a multitude of swim attire.

I get a few heated stares from some of the guys and ignore them as I head for an empty chair by the pool where I spot some sunscreen. I'm black haired, bright eyed, and so pale despite being half Chinese that my friend KeAnna jokes that instead of tanning, I turn translucent.

A joke, obviously, but she isn't far off. I was cursed with zero melanin, so the sun and I have never exactly been friends. Growing up, in the summer I would tell Zheng he was born selfish since he stole it all from our mom before I even had a chance. So unfair. A few hours outdoors and he turns a golden color that makes him look like a modern-day East-Asian Apollo. Meanwhile, I go from white to pink to red in a matter of minutes if I don't slather myself at least in SPF80.

After squirting some sunscreen in my hands, I massage it into my arms and legs when a shadow falls over me, blocking out some of the harsh rays from the sun.

"Want me to get your back?" A masculine voice asks, and I turn to find Deacon behind me, a luminescent purple drink in hand and a hesitant smile on his face.

"Oh, hey. What are you doing here?" I ask, and lift a hand over my eyes to see him better. He's wearing black swim shorts and no shirt, and has on mirrored sunglasses so I can't make out his eyes. His rune tattoos stand out against his skin, and for some strange reason I have the urge to trace them. An urge I definitely do not act on.

"I'm in Alpha Ze," he tells me. "Fae are supposed to mix and mingle too."

"Ah, it all makes sense now."

He tilts his head to the side. "What does?"

"That cocky charismatic charm of yours that you're able to flip on and off whenever you like. I thought it might be a Fae thing, but it's really a frat thing. Nice chatting this week, by the way. Coffee was great," I tell him and he grimaces. After we ran into each other I thought, I don't know, that we'd actually try the whole friend thing, but I guess when he realized he'd be stuck in the friend zone he didn't want to waste his time. Or maybe he decided shifters weren't really for him and he'd rather stick to his own kind. Not that I can blame him there. I prefer the company of my own kind too when given the choice.

What bothered me though, was we never talked after that day and in class, he wouldn't even look at me. If he wanted me to get the hint, I heard him loud and clear. I just wish he wasn't such an asshole about it. I don't understand why guys can't just be friends with a girl. Why does it always have to be something else?

"About that..." He rubs the back of his neck and is silent for a beat before dropping down on the lounge beside me.

# Chaper Eleven

## Meiying

Deacon massages his throat and I get the feeling he's working his way up to telling me something I'm not going to like to hear. When the seconds turn into minutes, I shift my focus back to applying my sunscreen. Seriously, if I don't, I will fry. Not even shifter genes keep me safe from that, which is a bit ridiculous if you ask me. I mean, I'll heal just fine, but something about sunburnt skin makes me itch like ants are crawling all over me, and if I can avoid that unpleasant sensation, I will.

"I didn't mean to ghost you."

I put a little lotion on two fingers and massage it through the crisscross ties running down the front of the suit. I look ridiculous doing it, but a girl has to do what a girl has to do.

"So why did you?" I ask. My feelings aren't hurt by it, to be honest. I have plenty of friends and I'm not actively searching for more. I guess I mostly just find it annoying. I don't get why guys only see value in women if there's a chance of them getting laid. It's bullshit if you ask me. The Pack doesn't work like that and I've never been able to wrap my head around why other factions do.

"Look, I don't want to cause drama and shit."

I wait. I don't know what he's looking for from me, but I'm not going to help him out here. He approached me, so if this is going to be an issue—him talking to me—he's just as welcome to walk away.

"A few of the guys on the Infernum team aren't cool with the idea of us hanging out," he tells me and I stiffen. Dammit. Because, of course, Desmond didn't forget about the silver marks after he left the classroom. I mean, he had no problem forgetting me, but not Deacon. Not when it gave him the opportunity to be an even bigger asshole.

I grind my teeth together and ask, "Was it all three of them?" If it was, then I have three wolves to get back at instead of just the one.

Deacon shakes his head, "I don't think so." He pauses. "Not in the beginning at least. I think only our Reaper has a problem with it, but those three are tight—"

"Yeah," I sigh. "I know."

We're both quiet for a moment.

"He your ex or something?" Deacon asks.

I snort. "Definitely not. We've never dated and trust me when I say, we never will."

One dark brow raises over the rim of his glasses. "You sure about that? The way Pierce was acting, it's the way a jealous ex would be if he caught someone sniffing around his girl."

My lip curls. "First, I'm not a dog. No one is sniffing anywhere.

And second, yes, I'm sure about that. I've known him since we were kids. We belong to the same Pack. We're all sort of in the same friend group and he's housemates with my older brother. He takes the term 'overprotective' to the extreme." They all do. They're the bonus brothers I never asked for. Well, except for Desmond. I mean, I still didn't ask for him. That part is true. But of all the guys, he is the one I most definitely do not see as a brother. Even more so after what happened between us earlier this week.

*Asshole.*

Deacon nods, and I hate that I still can't see his eyes, so I decide to do something about it. Reaching up, I pluck the shades off his face, folding them down and setting them beside me.

"So, what did those three knuckleheads do, exactly? I'm assuming threats were involved, or did he go on a power trip and threaten to have you removed from the team?"

A flash of fear appears on his face, but it's gone a second later. Shit. Desmond really got to him. I know he can be scary, but Deacon is a Fae for chrissakes. He shouldn't just roll over and play dead when the big bad wolf comes knocking. I thought his kind were built of stronger stuff.

"No. Not that. I'm still on the team." His Adam's apple bobs as he visibly swallows. "He can't get me kicked off, anyway."

I inwardly groan. Why are the pretty ones so dumb? Desmond could absolutely get Deacon removed from the team. All it would take is one phone call to his parents, a sizable donation, and boom. Goodbye, Hellbound U. Hello, human community college.

I decide not to tell him that because he seems a little freaked out as it is. If you didn't grow up in Sun Valley, then it's safe to assume you don't know how big of a deal Desmond's family is. Deacon probably knows who the Pierces are, the same way everyone in the states knows who Bill Gates is. But, if you saw him walking down the street, you'd probably walk past him none the wiser, and it's not like you'd know who his kids were or what they looked like. Desmond's parents are a lot like that. They're the most visible shifter family in the nation, using their status and wealth as a means to show the humans that the monsters can be just like them too.

"Yo, D!" someone shouts, pulling Deacon's attention. "Is that her? The chick you got your ass kicked for?" He gives me a heated look, biting his fist. "Damn, man. I get it."

"Reed, fuck off," Deacon snarls right as I give the guy a one-fingered salute.

"Come on, man. No need to be like that. I was just complimenting your girl. I'd tap that for sure." He makes a thrusting motion with his hips and Deacon groans, covering his face with his hand.

"I apologize on behalf of my idiot frat brother. You probably won't believe me, but he's actually a pretty cool guy when he's not wasted like he is now."

Yeah. Not so sure about that, but I leave it alone.

"He said you got your ass kicked. That was because of me?"

He sighs. "It's nothing. Can we drop it?"

Uh, no. No, we cannot drop it. I told Desmond it was an accident. Obviously he didn't let it go, but I'd expect him to throw his weight around. Maybe threaten Deacon or try to intimidate him somehow.

Physically assaulting him is taking it to another level. Why is he so riled up about this? And now that I think about it, I look down at Deacon's hands, noting the absence of the rings from his fingers.

I sigh. "I'm going to need a play-by-play. I can get that from you or from some of your brothers who, by the sounds of it, are in the know. Up to you."

His jaw flexes, but instead of telling me what happened, he asks, "Did you lie and tell him I hurt you?"

"Excuse me?"

He turns narrowed eyes my way. "I've gone over what happened in my head a few times and Desmond said I hurt you. Left a mark. But," he shakes his head, "I never hit you. I don't hit women. I'm trying to figure out why you'd tell him otherwise."

His nostrils flare and damn, he looks pissed. All over again, I get the feeling he isn't someone safe. It's like he hides this dangerous edge about him under layers of confidence and charisma.

"Well?" he snaps.

I lift my arm in answer. When he sees the still darkened marks, he grabs my arm and tugs it closer, taking me with it since, well, it's sort of attached. I all but fall into his lap, but he doesn't even notice. His eyes lock on my skin. Flexing his fingers, he touches each one before cursing under his breath.

"Shit. I thought he was just being an asshole. Shifters heal so quickly, I didn't think ..."

"Silver poisons. It burns our skin like a hot iron and sinks its claws into our bloodstream. So yeah, we heal quickly, but that doesn't mean we don't feel pain, that injuries don't still hurt. And for the record, I told him you didn't mean to hurt me. That it was an accident and you must not have realized your rings were branding my skin each time you touched me."

He hangs his head. "I know shifters have an aversion to silver. But I wasn't thinking. Silver acts as a conductor for my magic. It lets me better focus it so it pours from my hands and not from my entire body. I wasn't thinking when I reached out for you."

He sucks on his teeth. "I get why you got all jumpy after that when I tugged on your hand. I," he pauses, "it wasn't on purpose. I mean, leaving those marks. Hurting you. I am not that guy. I'm *trying* not to be that guy."

"Have you ever been that guy before?" I ask, needing to know if he's safe. If he's someone I should be careful around. I'm confident I could take him if I needed to, especially if I shifted into my between form, but I don't like having to be on my guard twenty-four-seven.

He shakes his head, and I exhale a breath of relief. "No. My old man is, though. He likes inflicting pain on people and seeing how much they could take before sacrificing them for his magic. But I won't ever allow myself to become a monster the way he is." There is steely determination in his voice. "I'm sorry. We're getting into deep shit when we barely know each other." He chuckles, but it's forced.

"It's all good. And thanks. For the apology, I mean."

He nods.

"I still want that play-by-play, though," I remind him.

I wait. He tips back his beer, his throat working as he takes a long pull.

"Stalling will get you nowhere."

He grunts and then shakes his head. "We had some words. It's over now."

"Hey, Reed?" I call out. I stand and scan the backyard, looking for Deacon's frat brother who brought this all up in the first place.

Deacon hisses. "Meiying, drop it."

"Yo!" Reed hollers.

"I have questions." I nod my head and indicate for him to come over. He says a few more words to the guys he was talking to before slapping one on the back and heading our way.

"Meiying—" There's a warning in Deacon's voice. It's cute. I mean if I don't listen when Desmond gets all growly, why would I listen now?

"You're welcome to tell me yourself," I remind him.

He presses his lips into a firm line. Alrighty then.

As soon as Reed is close I say, "What happened with Deacon and Desmond Pierce?"

Reed whistles. "Aw, man. That was some rough shit." He ignores the death stare Deacon is giving him and dives into his recount of Tuesday's events. Desmond getting in Deacon's face. Choking him. How Deacon nearly passed out after Desmond wolfed out on him.

Deacon is quiet the entire time, chin down and shoulders slumped.

"And then the other guy, what's his name again?" He snaps his fingers before answering his own question. "Jordy! That's what all the jocks call him. So Desmond is walking away, point made, am I right?" He wiggles his brows. "When his buddy, Jordy, starts talking in Spanish and punches Deacon while he's still on the ground. It was fucking savage."

Deacon groans. "Thanks for the recount, man. Appreciate it."

Reed misses the sarcasm in Deacon's voice.

"Jordy punched you?" I ask. Now, that surprises me the most.

Deacon sighs. "Yeah. I don't think he or Rafael knew why Desmond was in my face. They were trying to haul him off me at first. Talk him down and shit." His mouth tightens. "After Desmond made his point, he warned me off you and mentioned that." He points his beer toward my arm. "Chavez blew a gasket and clocked me. Now that I see it, I can't say I really blame him. I'd be pissed too if someone hurt a girl I cared about."

"I'm sorry. The guys can be overprotective."

"It's all good now. Like I said. It's done."

"Fuck no, it's not. D, you haven't told her about practices, man."

"Shut the fuck up, bro," he grinds out. But Reed is drunk, making him oblivious to Deacon's warning.

"What's going on in practice?"

It's Reed who answers. "Deacon is getting his ass handed to him. All day, every day. Desmond is putting him through the ringer and defense isn't protecting him. He's getting sacked damn near every play he runs. It's fucking brutal."

My eyes widen. "You're kidding?" Why wasn't his team watching his back? Deacon and Desmond both played Reaper, which is the most vital position on the field. If your Reaper is taken out, your chances at winning plummet, and you have to score three times as often to make up for the loss.

Anyone can score in Infernum, but a Reaper scoring counts for three points, whereas everyone else's only counts for one. The Reaper is the primary scoring player. Wolfbacks and Bloodhounds are the offensive players. Their job is to clear the field for the Reaper through tackles, and also try and get the other teams Reaper out by pegging them with a death ball.

"No. And we're not practicing with death balls so ..." He lets the sentence trail off and I inwardly flinch. If defense isn't protecting him and they're not practicing with death balls, probably to build up strength and stamina, then that means he's taking a lot of physical punishment.

Wolfbacks and Bloodhounds have one death ball a piece—a baseball sized sack filled with a fine red powder that explodes on contact to mark whoever is hit. They can throw them at other teams' players at any time, but they only get the one the entire game, and if they fail to hit their mark, the death ball is lost. It's the only way to eliminate other teams' players during the game, and the fatality in Infernum only lasts one quarter, so it's usually smartest to use them on a Reaper since that's each team's most valuable player. And when those run out or are being saved for later use, the next best bet is to tackle the Reaper again and again until he stops getting up.

With that in mind, they're supposed to be the most protected. Each team plays with eight players on the field. Two Wolfbacks which play forward. The Bloodhounds which keep to the middle of the field. Your Reaper. And three Lion guards. They're your pit and Reaper defenders. Two usually stick close to the Reaper and the third lingers back by the pit—A one foot by one foot hole in the ground that acts as the Infernum goal. To score, you have to sink your ball into it. And at the start of the game, a new ball shoots skyward out of it. The pits are magically enchanted, so the kind of ball that is ejected each quarter varies and is meant to challenge all factions at different times. There are silver balls which are coated in silver alloy poisonous to shifters. Fire balls which are ringed in green fire. They burn like hell but unlike traditional fire, won't engulf a vampire on contact, making them not safe per se, but safer for a vamp to handle. Earth balls are made of solid stone and are said to weigh two hundred pounds. And bright balls are spheres of magical light that blind anyone within three feet, making the player rely on their other senses to make it to the pit.

"So you're getting sacked a lot?" I ask.

Before he can answer, his friend jumps in for him again. "He wishes it were just sacks." He chuckles darkly. "Five plays in on day one and it dawns on Deacon that protection is bad and it's staying bad. He starts to scramble when he gets the ball. Man doesn't want to get hit and he's fucking up the score, which is pissing everyone off even more. They're hitting him with magic attacks now or using the full strength of their faction."

Deacon is rigid, every muscle in his face drawn tight. He doesn't like hearing this.

"This shit goes on for three days," Reed says, waving three fingers in the air. "And then out of nowhere, Pierce takes to the field, smacks our boy here upside the head, and tells him, '*You're fast. Play faster. Trust your feet.*' It was solid advice, but Deacon isn't having it. He's pissed."

"Can you blame me?" Deacon snaps.

Reed lifts both hands in the air. "Nope. I'd be an asshole, too. Maybe not to the dude's face like that, but..." He shrugs. "Anyway, Hunt is mouthing off. He tells Pierce he's playing dirty, fucking with his protection, and damn, you should have seen the look on Pierce's face. He told Deacon if he wanted protection, give them someone worth protecting. And if he doesn't like getting hit, then go play fucking tennis with the humans."

I wince. Desmond's never been one to mince words. "That was harsh."

"But effective," Reed smirks.

I turn to Deacon, who's still glaring, but when he sees me looking, he nods. "It did the job," he sighs. "Got my head out of my ass and back in the game."

"And made you a damn better Reaper. Deacon learned in three days what takes most Reapers years to figure out, and he's not buckling under the pressure. He's playing smart. He's not relying on anyone else to save his ass either."

"Has Des backed off? Are the lion guards helping you out now?"

Deacon snorts. "No. I'm still on Pierces' shit list. But now," he shrugs, "I do my part to not get taken out."

"So, he's still getting hit a lot." Reed supplies, and Deacon shoots him another glare. "Hey, don't get pissy with me, my friend. You're just mad because that asshole made you a better player and you don't like it."

"Yeah, whatever." Deacon finishes his beer and stands. "I need another drink. You?"

"Uh, sure." He nods, and I watch as he heads over to the coolers the girls placed near the pool. Once he's out of earshot, I turn back to Reed and ask, "What's he going to do? Getting sacked in practice is one thing, but he can't be left defenseless in a game. He'll end up seriously hurt."

Reed gives me a sobering look. "I think he's hoping you can help him out with that."

Me? What the hell was I supposed to do?

# Chaper Twelve

## Desmond

**Z**heng's riding the line again, his beast fighting him from the inside to break free. He isn't sleeping and he's jumping at loud sounds. I know what's coming and I'm trying to head it off, but the asshole standing in front of me isn't making that easy.

"Bro, we had a deal?"

Zheng throws on his leather jacket and swipes his keys off the table, heading for the front door.

"I'm not going to do anything stupid," he assures me, but we both know that's a lie.

"You heard what the doc—"

His jaw clenches. "I'm going to live my life. Okay? Can you get on board with that, man?"

I grind my teeth together. This is a bad idea, and he knows it. His beast is fighting for control and going out right now is a bad fucking idea, but I can see by the look in his eyes I don't have a shot in hell of talking him out of it. I never do. Not when he gets like this.

Liu is a walking, talking stick of dynamite just waiting to explode. When we were kids, he was always a self-destructive shit, but adult Zheng is on a whole 'nother level. We've all got baggage, but the shit Zheng needs to unpack is traumatic as fuck, and I only know the half of it. But we made a deal. I'm not about to let him weasel out of it.

"When you stop being a lying sack of shit, maybe." I shrug and wait to see how he responds. It can go one of two ways. Brotherhood will get the better of him and he'll back down. Nine and a half times out of ten, he's true to his word, and he hates being called a liar. Addicts are liars, and Zheng refuses to be one of them like his human father.

I see the flicker in his eyes. The moment of hesitation at my words and then... *fuck.* There's that other half. The times when he decides not to give a fuck because he's too far up his own ass to think straight and his beast is riding him too hard that he can't even hear the voice of reason.

"Zheng—"

"You know me," he says, and there's a plea in his voice, so I nod. "You know I've been clean. For two years I've stayed clean. No missteps. I've stayed on the fucking wagon, man."

"I know." Which is why what he's doing now is pissing me off. Drugs shouldn't affect shifters, but fae ones do and Zheng had a tumble with them none of us wants a repeat of. He nearly went rogue while on the stuff, and if he had, we would have lost him to his beast. There's no coming back from that, not when you give in to your animal so completely that you lose your humanity in the process.

It's like he forgot what the first year getting clean was like. The depression. The withdrawals. He was so fucking sick back then he had to take a full semester off. It was dangerous as fuck getting on the stuff to begin with, and doubly so getting off.

And now he wants to risk it all for a party and a piece of ass. I shake my head. This was a mistake.

"It's a pool party. There will be magicked brews, but no drugs, and we both know brews were never my problem."

No. It wasn't. Zheng's issue started as a little recreational elderflower until he fucked up. Got behind the wheel while high as a kite on supernatural drugs and wrapped his car around a tree, injuring his passengers—Rafael, Jordy, and me. Shit got ugly after the accident, and we didn't speak for close to a year after that. It shouldn't have been as bad as it was. We're all shifters, able to heal at an accelerated rate, thanks to our animals, but we all experienced several breaks, and by the time help arrived, our bones had healed at wrong angles and our injuries needed to be rebroken and set to prevent permanent damage. It fucking sucked.

What none of us knew at the time though, was that Zheng was almost kicked out of the Pack for it. He was a minor driving while under the magical influence and had over forty grams of elderflower on him when Pack healers picked us up. We don't mess with Fae drugs. Or any drugs, for that matter. It's strictly forbidden because of the risk of going rogue. We have to stay in control of our beasts at all times.

The accident also took place on human streets outside of Pack territory, so the HPED got involved and wanted to charge Zheng with a class C felony. Our Alpha couldn't make it go away. Not entirely. So the HPED offered Zheng a deal, and our Alpha accepted it on his behalf.

It was a shit deal, if you ask me. It required Zheng to become an informant for the HPED on all things supernatural, so long as they didn't pertain to shifter secrets or the Pack.

Big fucking mistake.

Rafael's dad was Alpha back then and made the arrangements. If Rafael ever found out, there'd be hell to pay, which is why even after shit was smoothed out between us all, Zheng never mentioned it.

Shit should have been straightforward. On paper, Zheng was supposed to tip the HPED off about corner dealers selling magicked drugs to kids at our school, but what really happened was they forced him into the deep end. They had a sixteen-year-old shifter worming his way into the paranormal underworld, and shit got messy.

I don't know all the details of everything that went down. But I know shit escalated with drugs. Elderflower turned into Fae Fires and that turned into Bloom Crystal. There was a girl Zheng refuses to talk about. And a drug deal that went south that he got caught up in. He hasn't shared the full story, but on top of the addiction, he got a nice case of PTSD. When he's having an episode things get heavy. The way he reacts, you'd think he'd been to war. I guess in a roundabout way he has. But it's dangerous as fuck for anyone around him when he drops into one of those spells.

Zheng worked on getting clean before we moved in together, and I helped get him out of the informant program as soon as I learned he was in it. Fuckers didn't want to let him go, but I made sure they realized they didn't have a choice. Sometimes it pays to be a Pierce. This was one of those times.

But the road to recovery is a long one, and staying clean isn't the only thing Zheng needs to worry about. "Access to drugs isn't what I'm worried about. I know you're good." The first six months were rough, but the next year and a half were solid.

Zheng lets out an exasperated sigh. "I'll be fine."

"You jumped me when I slammed the back door earlier."

He closes his eyes, hands fisted at his sides and skin rippling with the urge to shift. Something he better not fucking do right now. "You caught me off guard."

Yeah. I've been doing that a lot lately. It's why I've made it a point to be around as much as possible. I go to class, the field, and then straight home. I've met up with Zheng for lunch between classes all week, and when he's feeling up for it, he kicks it at the field and catches up on his schoolwork while he waits for me to finish up with Infernum practice.

It's not ideal. We don't do secrets in our crew. But this ... this is Zheng's damage. It's not my place to tell the others. Zheng will do that when he's good and ready, so for now, this is what works.

But part of why it works is because we avoid scenes like what Zheng is about to put himself in. Parties are loud. Rowdy. And shit is never clean when other factions are involved. People get into stupid shit and no, I don't think Zheng will slip up when it comes to drugs. He's worked too fucking hard for his sobriety. But this week he's been off, and I'm waiting for the other shoe to drop. I can sense how restless his beast is and it has me worried.

"There's going to be loud music. Probably shit with a heavy bass. People are going to be shouting. They're going to rub against you when you walk by. How do you think your tiger will react?" I'm not his dad or his Alpha. I'm not going to order him around, but he needs to see this for what it is. A bad idea.

"I'm going. You wanna babysit, be my guest, but I'm climbing the walls here, Des." He slams a palm to his chest. "I can't breathe, and I know I'm fucked up in the head right now, that my beast is teetering on the edge, but this is what I've come up with and I'm seeing it through."

I grab my phone and slide it into my back pocket. "Let's go, then."

Zheng's shoulders relax and we head out. He tells me on the way that the party we're headed to is at Kappa Eagle. Meiying's sorority house. *Shit.*

We haven't talked since the classroom. I'm a dick. She knows that already. This isn't some new revelation. But I took shit too far that day. And if Zheng finds out what I did to his baby sister, what I still think about doing to her, I'm fucked.

# Chaper Thriteen

## Meiying

"I see you're having fun," Quinn says, a smirk on her face as she moves to stand up beside me. "Any chance your hottie has a brother?"

I follow her eyes and see that she's ogling Deacon. "Not that I know of, but he's not my hottie. We just happen to have English together this semester, so you should go for it."

Her eyes bug out and she whips toward me. "Seriously? You wouldn't mind?"

I laugh. "Nope. He's all yours. Deacon isn't really my type."

She looks at me like I just spoke a foreign language. "Have you seen the guy?" she asks. "That fine specimen of a man right there is everyone's type."

"He's good-looking, I'll give you that. But..." I trail off.

"But? There are no buts." She places the back of her hand against my forehead. Then my cheeks. "Are you feeling okay? No fever, but

I'm worried about you. Maybe you should lie down. All this sun is getting to you. Can shifters get heat stroke? Oh my god, what if you're going blind?"

I smack her hand away. "I'm fine," I tell her with an exasperated breath. "I just don't really date and I'm not into Fae. They're always players." I hedge, not that I could care less whether Deacon gets around or not, but using Desmond's dig seems like a plausible excuse.

"You do realize you're a shifter, right? You guys are known for getting around and then some."

I shrug. "So, I'm a hypocrite. Sue me. Are you really going to stand here and continue trying to convince me to go for him, or are you going to take your fine witchy ass over there before one of our sorority sisters shoots their shot?"

"Oh, my God, you're right." Quinn fluffs her hair and adjusts her boobs. Yes, she actually shifted her girls around before glancing at me with an expectant look. "How do I look?"

"Hot! Go get him."

She gives an excited squeal before taking a deep breath and marching toward him. Deacon drifted back to his friend group a little while ago, giving me a much-needed respite after everything he and Reed had unloaded. A part of me wants to help. I feel a little responsible for what he's going through, but a bigger part of me really doesn't want to get involved. I don't want an excuse to seek Desmond out. If I do ... I don't know. But it isn't going to be good. I'm angry and a little hurt, though mostly angry, and my tigress wants to claw his eyes out. This is the second time something like this has happened between us, and both times he ghosts me. Woman and beast have had enough.

What the hell is his problem, anyway? I'm not asking for a relationship or even a repeat event. All I'm asking for is some human decency. It's really not too much to ask.

But, whatever. This is Desmond I'm talking about here. I turn and grab a water bottle from one of the coolers and head for the pool. There's a pink sprinkle, donut-shaped floaty with my name on it.

One of the Alpha Ze guys helps me maneuver my way onto it without jumping into the pool because not gonna lie, that water is cold, and I'm a cat. While natural tigers might like the occasional swim, I, personally, am not a fan.

I'm laying back, enjoying the music and chatter around me when something in the air shifts. I don't know how else to describe it. It's like an awareness comes over me that he's here without needing to see or scent him.

Sunglasses firmly in place, I turn my head to the side just in time to spot my brother and—would you look at that—Desmond, arrive.

For a second, a flash of panic hits me square in the chest and I look down at myself. Fuck. I'm dead. So dead. When Desmond sees what I'm—hold on. I cut that thought off and scoff. What am I even thinking? Fuck what Desmond thinks. Quinn is right. I look hot. No way in hell am I going to let that asshole shame me for wearing this suit. I'm going to own it.

I track their progress through the yard, grateful no one can see my eyes because I'm totally staring, and if I had to guess, my tiger is shining in my gaze.

Zheng, being the friendly guy he is, dives right in on the fun and joins with a few of the guys at one of the backyard games the girls must have set up. The one where you toss hacky sacks at an angled board and try to get it through the hole, only to make things more difficult, the hacky sacks are on fire so you have to move fast to avoid being burned.

"Hey, what's that game called?" I ask one of the guys swimming next to me. I'm not sure what his name is. He hooks his arms over the side of my floaty and looks to where I'm pointing. "Corn hole," he tells me, and then instead of swimming away, which was what I'd been hoping for, his eyes do a slow and obvious perusal of my body. "I'm Ignacio, but everyone calls me Iggy."

"Hi. I'm—"

"Meiying!" A familiar voice barks out my name and instantly my hackles rise. Well, that took longer than expected. *Not.*

I turn my head to find Desmond, arms folded over his chest and dark eyes ablaze with his wolf. He's not wearing sunglasses like virtually everyone else here, so I can spot his glare from the edge of the pool and offer him a little wave.

His nostrils flare. I shouldn't take pleasure in riling him up, but it's so damn easy.

Dressed in black jogger pants that taper at the ankle and a white crew t-shirt that hugs his broad shoulders and impressive chest, I have to fight the urge not to lick my lips. Has he always looked this good? Who am I kidding? Yes. Of course he has.

He's wearing his usual red sneakers, but he's changed his hair. For as long as I've known him, Desmond's kept it braided back over his scalp. Sometimes they're thick braids. Other times they're thin. But for the first time, there are no braids. Sometime this week he got his hair cut and damn, it looks good on him.

A line up and fade make his features appear sharper, and he's added a razor part design. Two parallel lines that start at his temple and slant up enough to form a peak before curving down and back. Almost like a lightning bolt.

"I didn't think this was really your scene." I keep my tone casual, my expression carefree, and I thank my lucky stars that I'm far enough away and downwind that my scent won't carry to him. As a hunter-born, his sense of smell is stronger than most, and he can pick up on emotional scents when he wants to. It's insanely intrusive, if you ask me.

People are watching our exchange, the girls already trying to figure out how we know one another. This is exactly why I didn't want him and the other guys here when I moved in. They draw too much attention. Most of the guys here are well built, but none of them has the impressive muscle mass Desmond has, his shifter genes and intense workout schedule giving him an Adonis-like body.

"Get out of the pool." His voice is hard and his tone is laced with the order of an Alpha.

Too bad he's not an Alpha. Asshole. "Pass. I'm enjoying myself right here."

I swear steam comes out of his ears and a snarl curls the edges of his mouth.

"Meiying—" There's a warning there. One I should probably listen to, but where is the fun in that?

"Desmond," I retort.

His jaw is tight, a vein bulging in his neck. This is too good. Alpha Ze guy—what was his name again? Oh, right, Iggy—is still clinging to my floaty, but his eyes keep bouncing back and forth from me to Des and then back again. I'm not sure what faction he belongs to, but it's clear he's not interested in messing around with a wolf.

"Hey." I draw his attention.

He turns, expression a little nervous. Well, shit. That won't work. I turn my smile up a notch and shift to my side, which gives him a better view of my breasts. "Sorry. He's so rude. I'm Meiying." I pick up where we left off, suddenly interested in chatting with the guy.

He swallows hard, eyes locked on my chest.

"So, what year are you?" I ask, and right as I'm about to trail a finger over his arm Desmond snaps, "Rojas. Off limits. Get your ass away from her."

Iggy jumps back as if he's been electrocuted and makes quick work of following Des's orders. "Yeah, man. Of course. I was just, uh, making conversation. You know?"

Desmond doesn't answer him. He gives Iggy a flat stare before dismissing him with a look that promises pain if he doesn't hurry the fuck up, and then he turns his attention back to me. "I won't ask again, Meiying."

I flip him off. There are a few muffled laughs from the yard, and I spot Deacon and Reed barely keeping themselves in check. Desmond sees them too. *Oh, shit.* He stalks in their direction. *Shit. Shit.*

Deacon sees him coming and squares his shoulders, nostrils flaring. The runes on his arms take on an ethereal glow, signaling that he's drawing on his powers. Double shit. He's not going to back down. "Des!" I paddle my arms to reach the pool's edge but wind up spinning myself in circles. Navigation on a giant donut is not as easy as it might seem, but one of the guys is nice enough to give me a push to the shallow end and then I'm off. I jump in the thigh deep water. Gah! Cold. And hop up the steps.

Desmond is in Deacon's face. No clue what he's saying, but it doesn't look like they're discussing the weather. Everyone is watching. Waiting for fists to fly. But yeah, no. Not happening.

I shove myself between the guys and push Desmond in the chest as hard as I can. He moves back a few steps, but only because he's willing to.

"Happy now? I'm out." He's glaring over my shoulder, still not looking at me. I turn and clear my throat to get Deacon's attention. His eyes shift and he looks down, and then all of a sudden I'm shoved back behind Desmond and he's all growly, saying, "Don't fucking look at her," like a possessive asshole. As if he has the right to say such a thing.

Then he's tearing his shirt off his head and shoving it down over mine. When my head pops out he helps me get my arms through the sleeves, and then he's back to shoving me behind him again. Whoa. He's seriously losing it right now. I've never seen him like this.

"I thought I made myself clear," he says, voice dipped low and threatening.

"What is your problem, man? She's not your girl. Back the fuck off."

Okay, so true, I am most definitely not his girl, but still, even I know that was the wrong thing to say. *Idiot.* It's like he *wants* to get his ass kicked again. The muscles of Desmond's back tighten, and wow, is it a good-looking back. Why have I never seen his bare back like this before? I mean I have before a shift, obviously. But, I've never taken the time to really look him over.

More heated words are exchanged, but I'm not really paying attention, too intent on tracing the lines between his shoulders and down his back with my gaze. That accomplished, I reach out and begin physically tracing the lines with my finger.

He stiffens. I don't let that deter me. I follow the path, applying light pressure, and some of the tension falls away. His muscles flex and Desmond takes a deep breath, no longer talking. I can sense his wolf, and it's almost like the beast sighs at my touch. My own animal is curious about the effect we're having on it.

When I reach the dip at the base of his spine I lean forward, resting my head against him. A tremor rolls through his body. His muscles twist beneath my palm and I can sense more than see that he's peering over his shoulder at me, but I refuse to look up, holding my breath as I wait to see his reaction. I should move away. Stop touching him. *Why am I touching him?*

That thought gets me out of my head and I jerk back, but he's there. He turns, grabs my still raised hand, and pulls me to him. Not in an embrace or anything like that. Desmond doesn't do public affection. Not that he's ever been affectionate with me. No. We fight. I guess we also sometimes angry kiss and dry hump, but whether that was a one off or will be a repeat event is yet to be decided.

So no, no embrace. But I'm right beside him. The heat from his bare skin seeps into me.

"What are you doing?" he asks. I meet his dark-brown stare. He doesn't look mad, at least not right at this moment. He looks... confused.

"Are you done?"

His brows pull together. "Am I done with what?"

"Being an asshole."

I open my mouth to add that he needs to stop laying into Deacon over nothing, but catch myself. He's calming down. I'd be stupid to say something I know will just piss him off again.

"You wanted me out of the pool. I'm out. Okay? Can we just ... I don't know, go inside? Cool down for a bit?"

He works his jaw, but nods and relief sweeps through me. Good. "Come on, then." I wait to see if he's going to follow before heading for the door when I catch sight of my brother right as he's turning.

He sees me. Smiles. Waves. But then he sees what I'm wearing. A wrinkle forms between his brows.

"What are you—" He eyes the shirt I'm wearing and then spots a shirtless Desmond behind me. "Why are you wearing his shirt?" There's genuine confusion in his voice and my heart starts to race because shit, um ... I go with the first thing that pops in my head.

"Because Desmond is an asshole." Yep. True and relevant. Score one for me.

"Huh?" Why does he sound confused? It's not like this is a new revelation.

I decide to elaborate. "He's a dick and made me put this on because my swimsuit is *in⋅ecent*." I make air quotes and glare at Desmond for exaggerated effect. "Did you tell him to cock block me?" I add, turning my glare on my brother. "Because that shit is not cool, Zheng. I know you guys are roommates and all, but I don't need babysitters at my own house."

His eyes widen and he gets this look on his face that screams *abort. Abort.*

I love my brother, but he's never really been one for confrontation. Not with me, at least. I happen to have a bit of a mean streak and a solid record for always getting revenge. What I just said basically implies I'll cock block him the rest of the year if he tries to cock block me. I should feel bad. The panic written all over his face is just too good.

"I wouldn't do that. I—" he sputters, and I fold my arm over my chest, lifting a single brow.

"Bullshit. You absolutely would."

He huffs and then seems to rally himself, which surprises me.

"Was it?"

"Was it what?"

"Indecent. Was the swimsuit indecent?" No. Maybe. Okay, yeah, I mean, have you seen it? It is a lot. But I wasn't going to admit that to my brother.

"It's a swimsuit." I argue. "Top. Bottom. The usual."

"Meiying—" He's glaring. At me. What the hell?

"What is going on right now. This is not how this," I wave at the space between us, "works. Desmond is an asshole. I yell at you and you apologize for him being an asshole. That's how this works."

He just stares for a beat and says, "Fine, let's see it. If he's wrong, I'll apologize for him being an asshole."

My eyes widen. "What? No!"

He gives me an are-you-serious expression. "It's a swimsuit. I've seen you in a swimsuit."

Desmond is shaking beside me fighting not to laugh. I shove him. "This is your fault."

He smirks. "Show him the suit, Baby Liu."

I grind my teeth together. Fine. I'm not embarrassed. I fucking rocked this swimsuit. With my eyes on his, I tug the t-shirt off. Desmond's eyes stay trained on my face, but I don't miss the hitch in his breath.

There's a gasp. "Jesus Christ." That was from Zheng. "Don't look at my little sister like that, you fucking perv." That catches both our attention, but when I look, Zheng isn't talking to Desmond, he's glowering at the guys he's been playing corn hole with. "She's only se—"

"Hey!"

He turns.

"Don't you dare," I warn. If he tells everyone I'm seventeen I will murder him. He must see that in my eyes, because he manages to keep his mouth shut and gives Desmond some weird look. Silent communication passes between them, and then the shirt is being shoved back over my head, only this time when my head pops out it's to see Zheng heading for the door.

I follow him, Desmond right behind me, and as soon as we're all safely inside Zheng whirls on me. "What the fuck were you thinking? Do you know what goes through those guys' heads when they look at you? Shit."

I wait. I'm not really sure what is happening right now. Zheng has always been protective, but he's also always let me do my thing. This is different. Almost like he's spiraling. I don't think all this anger is really about me. At least I hope it isn't.

"It's a swimsuit. I'm at a party in my own house I might add. I don't care how guys look at me or what goes on in their head. As long as they don't touch me without permission, I'm good. Virtually everyone in the Pack has seen me naked at one point or another. What difference does this make? You're overreacting—"

"Overreacting? Overreacting! Jesus Christ." He spears his fingers through his shaggy black hair.

"You said that already."

"Well, it warranted a repeat."

I smile a little at that. He takes a few deep breaths and then turns to Desmond and gives him a fist bump. "Thanks, man. I appreciate you looking out."

Desmond grunts and meets my stare. There's a warning, as if he's saying *on't you *are say a thing about what happene* in the classroom.

I glare back, my eyes conveying my own response. *I'm not an i*iot, asshole.*

"I'm gonna go down to the park. I need to get the image of my baby sister in that," he nods in my direction, "out of my head. I can drop—"

"I'm good. Go ahead. Meiying can give me a lift."

I scowl, but Zheng's not paying attention. "Cool man. I'll see you later back at the house."

He heads for the door, but at the last second Desmond stops him. "Yo!"

He waits until Zheng turns to face him. "If something comes up, you call. You hear me?"

More silent communication passes between them, and damn, is that sort of creepy. I know Zheng and Desmond are friends. Best friends now. But it's like they have their own language, and there is seriously something going on with my brother that definitely has nothing to do with my swimsuit.

# Chaper Fourteen

## Meiying

And then there were two. Zheng leaves to go boarding, leaving me and a very shirtless Desmond behind. Right. Clothes. He needs clothes. Which means I need clothes. Gah.

I head for my bedroom, conscious of Desmond's silent steps behind me. Once inside, I head for my dresser and pull out a pair of yoga pants and a sweater. I look down at the shirt. I don't want to give it back. It's soft and comfy and it smells like him. Like cinnamon and sandalwood and yum. *Oh my god.* I cannot believe I thought that. Not keeping the shirt. I am not that girl and no, I am not hung up on him. Just no. He's an asshole. An inconsiderate, domineering jerkface. And who the hell cares if my tiger wants to roll around in his scent? That's her problem, not mine. Nope.

I pull it over my head and hold it out to Desmond, who's just standing there. Staring. It's the first time I've gotten a good look at his front, and yeah, it's just as good as the back. Better actually, which is completely unfair.

His chest is wide, sculpted. He has abs that should be illegal. And those lines ... you know the ones.

I want to trail my fingers over those lines, lick his hip bone, stroke his abs. Wait. No. Fuck. I do not want to do any of those things. *Come on, Meiying, get it together.*

I take a deep breath through my nose. Not that it helps, because then I just smell him more, and it's so freaking good.

Dammit. I am not keeping the shirt and he really needs to put it on and leave. I cannot be around him right now. I think the sun addled my brain or something.

"Take it," I say, and give the shirt in question a little shake.

He's not looking at the shirt, though. He's looking at me. And the look in his eyes isn't an innocent one. It's the same look he gave me in the classroom. Heated. Hungry. Predatory. *Fuck.* I drop the shirt.

"Christ." He runs a hand over his head. "That thing is fucking indecent."

I look down at myself and yeah, he's not wrong, but neither was Quinn. I'm glad she offered me the swimsuit. Once I got over the shock of the thing, I decided I liked it. I don't care what anyone else thinks.

I've never had a hard time getting a guy's attention, present company not included, but I'm attractive in a cute sort of way. Not beautiful. Not hot or sexy. Just, cute. I have round cheeks, curly black hair, bright blue eyes and one of those faces that people look at and think to themselves, *she's cute.*

This swimsuit takes me from cute to sexy and I'm not going to lie, I like it. I like feeling sexy, and as much as I hate to admit it, I like the way Desmond is looking at me while I'm in it. Which, yes, I know that's bad. It's the sun. Totally blaming the sun for my crazy stupid thoughts right now, because I shouldn't like the way he's looking at me. In fact, I should be snapping at him for it. But I'm not. I need to steer us back onto safer ground.

"Thanks for the unsolicited opinion," I tell him.

"Put that back on." He nods to the shirt.

"Pass. I don't take orders from wolfholes."

His eyes narrow. "Put on the shirt."

"No. In case you didn't notice, Kappa Eagle is having a party. One I plan on getting back to and enjoying. You should have left with Zheng, but since you didn't, I'll be nice and let you borrow my car. But I'm going to go have fun." I'd breeze past him out the door if he wasn't still blocking it, but because he is, I lean back against my dresser and fold my arms over my chest to wait.

His jaw tics.

"Put on the shirt, Meiying."

"No."

"Dammit. Put on the fucking shirt."

"Make me, asshole."

Okay, that last comment, probably not a great choice of words. Desmond closes the distance between us. Capturing my hips in his hands, he jerks me to him.

"Why do you always have to fight me on shit?"

I give him an incredulous look. "You're kidding, right?"

His nostrils flare, his wolf flashing in his eyes.

"You do not get to dictate what I wear or do or anything about my life. You don't own me. Get that through your head." Something in me snaps. All my frustration from before, my anger and hurt at his dismissal, comes rushing to the surface. Where does he get off? "You think that, what, since we fooled around in a classroom that you all of a sudden get to make demands? That's not how this works, Des!" I shove at his chest. "Get the hell out of my way."

He shifts his stance, still blocking me.

"Desmond—"

"Put on the shirt or take off that suit. You're not going out where all those fraternity punks are in that."

I bite the inside of my cheek until I taste blood. "Fine," I snap.

Surprise flashes in his eyes and he takes a step back, giving me some space, but I'm not going to put on his stupid cinnamon smelling shirt. Since he wants me to take off the swimsuit, I'll take it off.

I grab the straps of the swimsuit and tug them down, pulling my arms out.

"What are you doing?"

Ignoring him, I push the swimsuit down past my ribcage, exposing my breasts.

*"Jesus Christ!"*

A small smile curls my lip and I shove the swimsuit down over my hips, letting it pool at my feet. I swallow hard, but refuse to be embarrassed as I raise my eyes to his. "Happy now?" My voice is surprisingly even, giving none of my nerves away.

Need flashes in Desmond's eyes as he drinks me in. Then, without saying a word, he turns, jerks my bedroom door open, and leaves, slamming it shut behind him.

My shoulders drop as a sharp ache spears into my chest. Rejected. Awesome.

My phone rings, but it takes me a minute to collect myself. I pick up Desmond's shirt from the floor and slip it on. Not because I want to wear anything that belongs to him, but because it's there. So what if he left. So what if seeing me naked made him run for the hills.

I dig my phone out of my bag. It's no longer ringing, but I can see it was my mom who called. I'll call her back later. I'm not really in the mood for one of her chats.

I consider going back to the party, but that doesn't sound appealing either, so instead, I drop down on my bed and crack open a textbook, telling myself that my decision to stay inside has nothing to do with Desmond. I just need to catch up on some homework.

# Chaper Fifteen

## Desmond

There are only a few blocks between the Kappa Eagle house and my place, so I walk, needing some time to clear my head and calm down my wolf. If I hadn't gotten out of there when I did, I would've done something I couldn't take back, not that the bastard living beneath my skin was bothered by it. And truthfully, I wouldn't regret it. I know that much. Taking Meiying and laying her down on her bed, sliding into her wet heat, yeah, that isn't something man or beast could ever regret. But it is something that will make shit complicated, and I can't do complicated right now. Almost to my street, I change course and head for the field instead. I need to run. My body and beast are wound up tight. I need to tire myself out and get Meiying out of my head before I find myself turning around and going back to her to finish what's been started.

Seven miles in and I still can't get the image of her naked body out of my mind. Sweat drips down my back, my calves burn, but I keep up the pace. Two more miles and my chest is heaving, but I still see her perfect tits. Her tiny waist. Her bare pussy. Running isn't going to cut it. My wolf is buzzing, the urge to claim the girl who isn't mine, could never be mine, thrums through me.

I jog off the track and head for my place. Maybe a cold shower will help.

When I reach my door, I notice Zheng's ride in the driveway, which means he's home. *Goo*.

"Hey, man. You good?" I ask as soon as I see him.

He looks up, eyes bloodshot and unfocused.

I curse. "What happened?"

He shakes his head.

I grab a water bottle from the fridge, uncap it, and bring it back to him. He accepts it but doesn't take a drink. "Bro, you're freaking me out. What happened?"

His hands flex. "I freaked out, alright."

"I'm gonna need you to give me a little more information."

He hangs his head, no longer meeting my eyes. "A car pulled up to me while I was driving. They had music going. I—" He swallows hard. "There were gunshots in the song. I didn't think. Just fucking panicked."

Shit. "But you came home? You're good? Nothing else happened? You didn't shift while driving?"

He exhales a harsh breath. "Yeah. I'm good. Just freaked the fuck out, but I maintained control of my beast." Okay. Good.

"Why didn't you call? I would have come back sooner." I rub the back of my neck. He can't keep going like this. He needs help. Like real, professional help from Pack healers and our Alpha. More help than I can give him. "I think you should see someone—"

"I'm not talking to a fucking shrink."

I open my mouth to argue with him. Our Pack therapists aren't regular shrinks. They can help him with the trauma and his beast, but a phone buzzing halts my response. Zheng frowns down at his phone, the thing still buzzing.

"Who is it?" I ask.

He shakes his head. "No clue." He lifts the phone to his ear and answers. "Hello?"

"I'm gonna grab a quick shower," I tell him and head down the hall. I make it quick and cold. Enough time to wash the sweat from my body and erase the images of Meiying from my head so my dick calms the fuck down and my wolf stops clawing beneath my skin to get to her.

That finished, I throw on a clean pair of clothes and head back to check on Zheng.

He still has the phone to his ear, but all the blood has drained from his face as he listens to whoever is talking.

"You okay, man?"

It's like he doesn't even hear me. His eyes fill with moisture and my chest seizes. *Fuck.* His hand falls away from his face, the phone still cradled in his palm. Whoever is on the other line is still speaking, but Zheng's no longer listening. I reach for the phone and he relinquishes it without comment.

I bring it to my ear right as he drops his head in his hands, a choked sob wracking his entire body mixed with the mournful yowl of his tiger.

"Who the hell is this?" I snarl.

There's a pause. "Are you related to Mr. Liu," a calm voice asks almost hesitantly.

"I'm his roommate. What's going on? What did you say to him?" He's not in the right headspace to deal with whatever shit this is right now.

The guy on the other line clears their voice. "I'm sorry to be the bearer of bad news. I was explaining to Mr. Liu—"

"Zheng," I correct.

"Right. I was explaining to Zheng that there's been an accident." I wait. "His... his mother was in a car accident on the highway earlier today. There was a pileup, and while Ms. Douglas was able to stop before colliding with the vehicle in front of her, the eighteen wheeler behind her wasn't able to do the same."

Fuck.

"Is she okay?"

He's quiet for a beat, and I look down at Zheng. He's hunched over, elbows on his knees and hands on the back of his head. If she was okay, he wouldn't be like that.

"We weren't able to get to her in time. She ... she never made it back to the South Atlantic Pack Compound. I'm very sorry."

"What the hell do you mean you didn't get to her in time?" I bite out, and it's Zheng who answers, his voice dejected.

"She was pinned and bled out. She couldn't free herself, so the Lyc-V in her system kept trying and failing to heal her until it burned out. She's gone."

"What?" I ask him, eyes wide before repeating into the phone, "What? She's dead?"

Zheng flinches.

"I'm sorry. She's gone. Zheng Liu is listed as her next of kin. She was a new addition to our Pack and I was contacting him so we can proceed with the next—"

"No. He's not dealing with that today. He just found out his mom is gone. Everything else can wait."

"Sir, if I—""No. You can call back in a few days. Give the man some time to grieve and don't you dare make any fucking decisions about her body." I hang up and toss Zheng's phone onto the sofa beside him.

"Hey." He's not looking at me. "What do you need, man? What can I do?"

He hiccups and then gets to his feet.

"Whoa. Slow down. Where are you going?" He grabs his keys and heads for the door, but I block him. "Zheng—"

"I have to tell my sister. *Shit.* How am I supposed to tell her? How do—"

Fuck. I didn't even think about Meiying. Shit. Shit. Shit. "Okay. It's okay. You don't have to do that right now. We have time."

"Yeah, I do," he shouts, tears tracking down his face. I've never seen him like this before, and fuck if I know how to fix it. This is not something he can handle right now. Already I can feel the beast inside him calling to my own. Bloodlust rises in him, searching for a way to deal with his grief and pain. "She needs to know. She'd want to know.

Now. Not tomorrow or in a few hours. She needs to know now. But how the fuck am I supposed to do that, Des? She's my baby sister and I have to tell her but—"

I nod my head and grab him in a tight embrace. He clings to me like his life depends on it, hands fisted in the back of my shirt. "I get it, man. But you're still processing shit right now and your beast is already on edge. You can't drive like this. Just...sit down for a few, okay. We'll sort this out."

His shoulders shake, the urge to shift consuming him. "She needs to know, man." His voice is hoarse.

"I'll tell her. You stay here and I'll tell her."

He pulls back and runs his hands through his hair, tugging on the strands as he begins to pace.

"You're cool with that? You don't mind?" he asks, not looking at me.

"I got you. I'll tell her. You stay here. I'll have the guys—"

"I don't need a babysitter," he grinds out.

"No, you don't. But you just lost your mom and you don't need to be alone right now either."

He shakes his head, about to argue.

"What about Isa?" I ask. They've always been close, and she lost her mom a few years back. She'll know how to help him get through this while I … shit. I don't know how I'm going to break this to Meiying.

"Just, Isa?" he croaks.

"Yeah, man. Just Isa."

A nod.

"Okay. I'll call her. Just sit down. Okay?"

Another nod.

I pull out my phone and make the call. An hour later, there's a knock at our door and I let her inside.

"Hey. How's our boy doing?" she asks, voice low.

I peer over my shoulder at the boy in question. "He hasn't moved since I called you. Hasn't talked, either."

She nods as I grab my keys. "Where are you going?"

I swallow past the lump in my throat. "He asked me to tell Meiying."

Her eyes soften and she places a hand on my arm. "Des, that's ... you shouldn't have to—"

"I know. But he can't, and someone needs to."

"I can call Joaninha."

I shake my head. "No. I've got this. You look after him. Don't leave him alone or let him go anywhere by himself. If you need to call Rafael to sit on him, do that, okay?"

She nods but..."I'm serious, Isa. He's dealing with some other shit right now, too. His mom dying is awful, but the timing couldn't have been worse. Do not leave him alone. I'll handle Meiying, but depending on how she handles things, I don't know what time I'll be back. If you have to leave—"

"I got it. He won't be left alone."

"Good." I leave Isa with Zheng and jump in my Escalade. When I pull up to her place, it hits me that I don't know what I'm going to say to her, so I sit there, my car idling. It's been a few hours since I left and I know she won't be happy to see me but... it doesn't matter. I told Zheng I'd have his back and tell her, so I'm going to do that. He shouldn't be the one to drop this bomb on her. I've got this.

There's a back entrance off the hall that leads to Meiying's room, so I put my ride in drive and head that direction. There's a chance Kappu Eagle's pool party is still in full swing. Parties like this are usually an all-day, all-night sort of thing. I don't want to see anyone and deal with their bullshit, so I'll slip into Meiying's room and wait for her there if she isn't inside already.

# Chaper Sixteen

## Meiying

**I**'m tired and hungry and decide to fix at least one of those problems by grabbing some lunch meat from the kitchen. Not my first choice, but I want meat, and this is what I have to work with. I probably should have put pants on, but I doubt anyone is going to come inside, and at least I bothered to slip underwear on before heading to the kitchen.

Desmond's shirt hangs down to the middle of my thighs, which is more than the swimsuit was covering. I should shred the damn thing. All I've had these past few hours is time. Time to think about how twisted up I am about a guy who clearly doesn't give a shit about me. I'm not this person, so why am I letting him get to me?

Decision made, I'm done letting him tell me what to do, or wear. I'm done giving a shit about his feelings or worrying about whether or not he's interested in me. I'm over it.

I'm going to focus on school. I'll date. Yes, I'll definitely date.

Maybe Quinn or one of the other girls can fix me up with someone and I can test the waters outside of the Pack. It's not like I'm looking for a mate right now or anything. I just need to get over whatever it is that I feel for that wolfhole.

The door leading to the backyard opens and Deacon steps inside.

"Hey," he says upon seeing me right as I shove a handful of turkey into my mouth.

I give him a wave and point to my mouth as I chew. He nods and a few seconds later I swallow. "Sorry. Didn't want to talk with my mouth full."

"No problem." He shifts uncomfortably.

"So..." I say.

"Yeah. Sorry. I was just coming in to use the bathroom."

I point down the hall. "First door on your right."

He nods. "Thanks."

"No problem." He goes to take care of business and I put the lunch meat package in the refrigerator before reaching in for a bottle of water and heading back to my room. I'm just passing the hallway bathroom when Deacon steps out. "Have fun," I tell him as I slip past.

"Oh, hey, wait up."

I slow my steps, but I don't stop entirely. "What's up?"

"I was hoping we could talk," he says.

"I thought we already did?" We pause outside my room and I hesitate to open it. I have a feeling if I open my door, he'll want to come inside, and I'm not sure that's a good idea. Deacon is nice, and hot. But I'm in a weird head space right now, and yes, I definitely want to get over whatever hang-up I have for Desmond at the moment, but I know myself. I'll do something reckless, like throw myself at the guy and just make a bigger mess out of things, which isn't fair to him. I need to find a guy not on the Infernum team. One Desmond can't screw with to get at me.

"We did, it's just—" My door swings open on its own. Correction, the jerkface standing inside my room opens it.

"Leave," he says to Deacon, right as I say, "What the hell are you doing in my room?"

Desmond doesn't look at me, his penetrating stare resting solely on Deacon.

"Look, man..."

Des shakes his head. "I don't have time to deal with you right now. You need to go. Now."

Deacon's shoulders are stiff as the guys stare off with one another. *Screw this.*

"Hi. I have a better idea. How about you both leave. That would be great."

Deacon looks down at me, a flicker of hurt in his eyes, and I wince. "Sorry," I tell him. "This one brings the bitch out in me."

That seems to satisfy him, but still, neither guy moves. I turn to Des. "Why are you even here?" I just decided I'm done with his crap and this is what the universe does? It'd be bad enough if he showed up on my doorstep, but in my room? Really?

Des looks down at me. "We need to talk."

I scoff. "Pass. I don't have anything to say to you." The universe can shove it for all I care.

He gives me a once over, a smirk curling the corners of his mouth when he sees I'm wearing his shirt. "That looks good on you." He fingers one of the sleeves.

I smack his hand away with my bottle. "Go home, Des."

"Meiying." There's a warning there, his wolf bleeding into his voice.

"She said go home, man. Take the hint and back off."

Surprising me, Des ignores him. Well, I guess that isn't really surprising, but I expected a verbal jab or maybe even a punch after that comment.

"I just want to talk—"

"No," I snarl. Honestly, I don't want to talk to either of them. I want to finish my cold lunch meat and then I want to go to bed.

"No?" He rears back incredulously.

"You heard me. No. You were a complete asshole today. You were an asshole last week. You keep fucking with me and for what? I'm tired of this game, Des. So, no, I don't want to talk to you. Not today. Not tomorrow. Just, go away."

He exhales a harsh breath and his eyes soften the slightest bit. "Meiying, I..." He pauses and turns to Deacon. "Look, I don't like you, but I need to talk to her about personal shit. So, you gotta bounce. Now."

Deacon's jaw tightens, but he nods. "Fine. But only if you get the team to stop fucking me over in practice."

"Done."

A nod. A handshake. And then Deacon leaves, and wasting no time, Desmond pulls me into the room and closes the door behind me.

"Just because you got rid of Deacon doesn't mean I'm going to talk to you. You can go, too," I tell him, setting my water down on the nightstand and shoving the last of the turkey into my mouth so I have an excuse not to talk to him at least for the next minute.

He sighs, and waits for me to finish chewing. Urgh. I don't want to talk to him, but I know he's going to try again, and now that I've had time to think, I'm done. I want off his merry-go-round.

"What part of go are you not understanding?"

His Adam's apple bobs. "It's about your mom."

A strangled laugh escapes me and I swing my arms wide. "What? What about her is so important that you had to come fuck up my night after already screwing up my day?"

He doesn't say anything, just looks at me like I'm a little crazy. And so what, maybe I am, but he made me this way. He's the one butting into my life. Interjecting himself where he doesn't belong, and now this.

"Well? What was so damn important that you couldn't just leave me the fuck alone?"

He's not leaving. Fine. I'll leave instead. I grab a pair of leggings— I'll throw them on in the car—slip on some sandals, and grab my phone and keys. Jerking my bedroom door open, I head for the side door.

"Meiying!" He calls my name, but I don't stop.

"Go home, Des," I call over my shoulder as I make it outside.

A few of the girls are outside hanging out on the picnic table. All of them looking my way as I exit the house, Desmond right behind me.

"Meiying, stop."

I flip him off over my shoulder and he growls. Actually growls.

Stupid wolfhole. I can growl too. I'd be happy to show him my teeth and sink my claws into his skin.

I'm almost to my car when he grabs me by the elbow, and I'm about to tear away from him when he bites out, "Your mom was in an accident."

"What?" I shake my head and pull away. "She literally called today while you were in my room earlier."

"Meiying," his voice is soft, eyes somber. A stab of pain hits me in the chest. No. He's wrong. I just talked to her a few days ago and she was fine. And she called earlier today. He doesn't know what he's talking about. I pull out my phone and punch in her number.

"Meiying—"

I hold my finger up, silently telling him to wait.

The call goes straight to voicemail. My stomach sinks. But no, that doesn't mean anything. Mom is forgetful. Her phone is probably dead. Once she charges it, she'll see the missed call and call me right back. It's fine. Everything is fine.

A notification flashes across the screen. I have a voicemail. I smack my forehead. Of course I do. She called earlier and left me a message. I enter my pin and wait for the message to start.

"Hey, sweetheart. I just wanted to check in on my girl. Hope you're having fun. I'll call yo—" her voice cuts off. There's the sound of tires squealing in the background. A shrill scream. The crunch of metal.

*Oh my Go*⸱! "Mom!" No. No. No. She has to be okay. She—

Desmond reaches out, but I slap his hand away. I need to find my brother. I need… I drop my phone and shove past him. My skin ripples with the urge to shift, my tiger wanting to protect me from the whirlwind of emotions trying to slam into me. "Meiying, stop."

I don't. I move for my car. I need to get away. I need a minute to just think. Strong arms band around me, turning me until we're face to face. "I'm sorry. I didn't know how else to tell you."

I shove against his chest, my tiger's claws piercing my fingertips and sinking into his flesh. He winces, but he doesn't budge. Instead, he holds me tighter against his chest, one hand cupping the back of my head and his wolf thick in his voice. "I'm sorry, kitten. I'm so fucking sorry."

I shake my head. "No!" My vision blurs, but I blink back the tears. *"Never let them see you cry, sweetheart."* Mom's words echo in my head.

I sniff and pull away using every ounce of shifter strength in me. This time, he's forced to let me go. "She's fine though, right? She's at a hospital or whatever? The Florida Pack healers got to her in time, right?" I rub my eyes with the backs of my hands.

He doesn't say anything. He just stands there looking at me with eyes full of what ...regret?

"Well?" I shout. "You can talk now. That's why you're here, right? Is she going to be okay?" I need to talk to my teachers. If Mom is hurt, she'll need someone to look after her. The lycanthropy virus in her veins should help heal up any of the major damage, but with it focused on that, her smaller injuries will be ignored, so she'll be sore. She'll want help, at least until she's back to feeling one hundred percent. I don't know how much time I can miss from school, but I'll figure that out later. Zheng will—*shit.* I need to talk to my brother. Does he know Mom was in an accident?

"Where's Zheng?"

"He's at home."

I frown. "Does he know Mom was hurt? I have to call him."

"He knows," Desmond says. "The hospital called him."

Okay. Good. She's at a hospital. That's good. But... "Why isn't he here? Why are you here telling me about my mom instead of him?" Anger floods my system and I latch onto it.

A tormented look flashes across his face. "He's having a hard time with the news. I don't..." he takes a deep breath, "he didn't know how to tell you."

"Is he packing at least?" I run through my mental to-do list. Pack some clothes. Notify my teachers that I have a family emergency. Book a flight to Florida. *Shit.* I don't even have the new address.

I'll figure that out once I talk to Zheng. I whirl around to go back inside. "Where are you going?"

"I need to pack."

"Meiying!"

"Desmond. I don't have time. If Mom is hurt, I need—"

"She didn't make it."

Something squeezes my chest and all the air whooshes out of my lungs. "W...what?" That's not possible. She's a shifter. We're tough. Hard to kill. A little accident should have been nothing. I mean, sure she'd have injuries, but to die from them ...

My knees shake and everything suddenly sounds far away.

Desmond steps toward me, but it's almost like he's out of focus. My vision is dark along the edges.

"What do you mean, she didn't make it?" My voice is quiet, almost like if I say the words too loud it will make them real. But they can't be real. Mom is fine. She has to be fine.

"I'm so sorry," he tells me. This time, I believe him. "Her car was crushed between two semi-trucks. The truck drivers were human and died on impact so there was no one to call for help. She ..." He hesitates. "She couldn't heal the damage before bleeding out. She was pinned and ..." He shakes his head.

"No." I press the palm of my hand to my chest. "She can't ... no. She can't just be gone. My mom," I choke back a sob. "No. She can't!"

Desmond steps closer, his hands reaching out almost like I'm a wild animal he's afraid to spook.

"It's going to be okay."

"No, it's not. It is not going to be okay. This is not okay!"

"Fuck. I know. I'm sorry. That was the wrong thing to say."

I can't breathe. I'm opening and closing my mouth, trying to suck in air, but it's like my lungs have stopped working. I'm like a fish stuck on shore and I can't fucking breath.

"Meiying? Fuck. Meiying!"

A large hand forces my head between my knees. I didn't realize I'd fallen to the ground. "Breath, kitten. In and out. That's good. Take another breath."

I try to focus on his words, but my chest hurts. It really really hurts.

He rubs circles across my back as I fight to get my emotions under control, but as soon as I manage to suck in a full breath, the tears come pouring out. A distant part of me is screaming to get it together. To push him away and find somewhere private to cry, but I can't move. I want to get up, but it's like the part of my brain that controls my limbs isn't working.

Strong arms scoop me up, and the next thing I know I'm nestled in Desmond's arms as he walks me to his Escalade. My entire body shakes like a leaf. *She's gone. She's really gone.* The realization slams into me like a freight train and a new wave of tears falls down my cheeks.

Desmond sets me down on the passenger seat. How he opened the door while holding me, I don't know. He reaches over me and secures my seat belt before cupping my cheeks, his thumbs wiping the tears on my face. "You're going to get through this," he says, his voice somehow both soft and firm.

I hear the words, but I don't believe them. How does anyone get through something like this? How does anyone recover after losing their mom?

The rest of the night is a blur. Desmond takes me to his place, but I don't remember the drive there or even getting out of his Escalade and walking inside.

Zheng is there. Isa too. She hugs me, I think. I'm not really sure.

And then, nothing.

# Chaper Seventeen

## Meiying

"Meiying?"

I blink sleep from my eyes. Sunlight filters in through the window and it takes me a minute before I'm able to turn my head and find the person who said my name, though the scent of cinnamon is heavy in the air so I know it's him even before our eyes meet.

"Des?"

He steps further into the room and I push up on my hands. I'm in bed. But, it's not mine. This bed is a queen, but I know mine in my room at the Kappa Eagle house is a full. "Whose bed is this?" I ask, not recognizing his or my brother's scent on the sheets. My throat is dry and my words come out raspy.

Desmond sits down beside me, placing a hand on my leg. "You're in our guest room. You fell asleep, so I brought you here." He shrugs. "Figured this would be more comfortable than the couch."

That makes sense. "Thanks."

He stares at me intently before asking, "Are you feeling okay? Did you ... did you want to talk?"

I scowl. "Why would I want to—" Last night comes rushing back to me and I suck in a shuddering breath.

"Meiying?"

Oh God.

"Hey. Hey!" He cups both sides of my face and my vision swims. I'm crumbling, and he gets a front row seat to the show. "It's okay."

I shake my head. No. It's not okay. My mom is dead. I'm seventeen and she's fucking dead.

I pull away from his touch and turn to my side, resting my head on the pillow as silent sobs wrack my body. *Don't let him see you cry.* I tell myself. *You fucke♦ that up yester♦ay. Don't make it worse. Hol♦ it together.* I try to draw on my beast for strength, but she's just as grief stricken as I am.

A rough hand rubs my back, but I pull away from the touch.

"Leave me alone," I whisper.

"Meiying." He sighs, and there's pity in his voice. It makes my tears fall faster. I don't want his pity. I just ... I want my mom.

Desmond leaves and I lose track of time after that. Day turns to night only to become day. It happens again and again, day after day. But I barely move from the bed. I get up to use the bathroom. Sometimes I get up and sit by the window and look outside. The last time I did that I fell asleep, only to wake as Desmond laid me back in bed.

He brings me water. A few times he's tried to get me to eat, but I'm never hungry. He's being nice to me and I hate it. This isn't how our relationship works. It's not helping me. It just makes it all worse. I've tried shifting into my tiger form to avoid conversation, but whenever I do that, Des shifts into his wolf, curls up beside me, and offers comfort in a way I have no chance of refusing. He's slept beside me most nights like that. His fur brushing against mine and his cold nose pressed into my side.

And every night when he pads into my room on all fours, I tell myself to snarl at him. To make him go away. But my beast never does. She leans on him in a way human me never could until we fall asleep, though he's always gone by the time I wake. I imagine he doesn't appreciate waking up to human me in the mornings since I tend to shift back in the middle of the night.

The door to my room opens and I know without rolling over to look that it's Desmond who's come inside. I haven't seen Zheng since I got here. He's dealing with his own grief. Neither one of us is really equipped to help the other right now. I feel like a shitty sister about that, but I'm pretty sure he feels like a shitty brother too, so I figure we're square.

"How are you feeling?" He always asks the same question, as if he doesn't already know the answer, so like all the other times, I don't bother to respond.

Desmond sighs and moves around the bed. He crouches down in front of me but I keep my eyes closed, hoping he'll take the hint and go away.

"You're not really asleep."

So? I want to tell him, but I stay quiet.

Another sigh. "The girls are here."

That catches my attention and I snap my eyes open. Desmond is eye level with me, his penetrating stare burning into me.

"They're worried about you. You're not responding to any of their texts."

"I don't want to talk to anyone," I whisper, my mouth so dry the words come out scratchy and raw.

He hands me an uncapped bottle of water. "Drink."

I shake my head. I don't want it.

"Meiying, drink the damn water or I'll hold you down and force it down your throat myself."

I glare at him, feeling mutinous. He waves the bottle in my face, his eyes daring me to push him.

"Fine." I pull myself up into a sitting position, making sure to keep the blanket tucked beneath my arms to cover my chest and take the bottle. Glaring at him, I swallow a few sips before giving it back. "Happy?" I ask and lay back down.

He grunts out a, "Yes," and places the water on the bedside table. "I told Isa and Jo you were dealing, but you know how they can be. They want to see for themselves that you're okay. I think they mostly want to make sure I haven't buried you somewhere."

I suck in a breath.

"Fuck. Bad joke. Ignore that." He shakes his head. "I just thought you'd want a heads-up before they came in."

He moves to stand, but I latch onto his wrist, stopping him.

I swallow hard. "Don't let them in."

His eyes soften. "They're worried about you. We all are. It's been four days Meiying—"

I shake my head. "Please. I... I can't."

He looks away, a tic jumping along his jaw. "You need the Pack. Isa lost her mom, too. She can help. Zheng's been spending a lot of time with her. Maybe—"

"No!"

He reaches down and tucks a strand of hair behind my ear, his fingers lingering on my cheek. "Okay. I'll tell them you need more time."

# Chaper Eighteen

## Desmond

"**S**he needs more time," I tell Isa, who gives me a worried look.

"It's been days," she says, like I don't already know that. "She needs her Pack. She ..."

"I know but she... she asked for more time. She's a tiger. Not a wolf like us. She doesn't have the same instincts. The same needs we would in her position. I'm not going to push her if she isn't ready."

Isa gives Joaninha a pointed look. "Maybe we can—"

"Jo, no. She said no. The answer is no." Neither girl looks happy with my answer.

"She has classes. She's—"

"I spoke with the admin. They notified her teachers of the situation."

Isa's eyes widen. "Oh. Wow. That was really thoughtful of you."

I grunt. "She's got enough to worry about." They both do.

Zheng's in the other room, phone held up to his ear. He's been handling funeral arrangements. Trying to get the body transported back here so he can host a funeral, but it's a slow-going process with a lot of paperwork and hoops to jump through since his mom officially joined the South Atlantic Pack, even if it was for less than a month.

"How's he doing?" I ask Isa.

She purses her lips. "As good as can be expected. He's talking about it which is good. He's not holding everything in and letting the pressure build but—"

He snaps the phone shut and throws it across the room, where it shatters against the wall. Yeah, he's handling shit well alright.

"Zheng?" I call, drawing his attention. "What's up?"

His chest is heaving as he fights to pull himself together. "I have to fly out to Florida. They won't release the body without me physically confirming it's her and signing off on some bullshit paperwork."

*Fuck.*

He runs his hands through his hair, his movements agitated.

"When do you need to go?" I ask.

"As soon as I can get there. I need to check flights and—"

"I got it."

He frowns.

"Peretti and Pierce has a company jet. I'll set it up. Just tell me when."

He swallows hard and nods. "Thanks, man."

"No worries. You want me to go with you?"

He looks at the door leading to the guest room, and I know what he's thinking. I don't like the idea of leaving Meiying alone any more than he does, but the thought of him dealing with this alone doesn't sit well, either. His beast is unsettled. Being hunter-born has me more attuned with the animals that lurk inside all our skins, and I don't like the grief and rage that all but bleeds from his pores these days. It's a dangerous mix of emotion that, even without the shit he was already dealing with would be a challenge for anyone to put a leash on.

"You should talk to her," I suggest, but he shakes his head. "I'm serious, man. She could use her big brother."

"How does that help her? I can't tell her it's going to be okay when I don't believe it myself, man. So what can I do? How can I fix this? Because as far as I see it, I can't." He hangs his head and walks out of the room, his shoulders hunched and head hanging low.

"One of us can go with him," Isa says. "You take care of our girl. They'll get through this."

I want to believe her, but it's been four days since I brought Meiying back to our place. Four days and she's barely moved from the guest room. She's not eating. She never talks. It's like the girl has gone catatonic. I don't know what to do, and Zheng's been fucking worthless, not that I can blame the guy.

He's either gone to Isa and Rafael's or he's locked in his room, and now he's going to fly to Florida. How long will that take? How much longer can Meiying hide before shit gets serious? Her body has got to be eating itself. Shifters need to consume insane amounts of calories to keep up with our rapid metabolisms. What she's doing now is slowly starving herself and her beast, and the Lyc-V in her system can't stave off the pain of that starvation much longer.

"Yeah, okay. I'll make some calls and set up his flight. Just ..." I hesitate, but someone else needs to know. I can't watch them both twenty-four seven. "Can I talk to you for a sec?"

Without needing to be asked, Joaninha excuses herself. "I'm going to head home. Call me if she changes her mind and wants to talk, okay?"

I nod and give her a quick hug goodbye, being careful of her swollen belly. She has a few months left, but already she looks ready to pop. When she's gone, I turn to Isa and consider what to tell her.

"Zheng's been dealing with ... things."

She raises a brow. "Yeah. His mom just died."

I shake my head. "More than that. I can't tell you the how or why. I shouldn't be telling you any of this so don't repeat it, not even to Rafe. Okay?"

She nods, worry crossing over her face.

"Zheng has PTSD."

She opens her mouth to ask a question, but I raise my hand to stop her. "Like I said. I can't tell you the why or the how. That's his story to tell when he's ready, but it's been getting worse and I'm genuinely concerned he could go rogue." She suckes in a harsh breath. "He wasn't handling it well before his mom died and now, well, it's not going to get any better. He's just ignoring one problem in place of the other, and eventually the other shoe is going to drop. He doesn't sleep enough, which makes his beast restless and irritable. He gets these night terrors where he wakes up panicked and drenched in sweat. There've been nights he's shifted and mistakenly attacked furniture, or hell, even me. And loud noises can set him off. Almost like a panic attack where he feels like the walls are closing in."

"Has he talked to anyone?"

I shake my head. "He won't see one of the Pack therapists or healers. I've tried, but he refuses. I just… you need to know what to look out for because he's getting worse, not better."

She nods. "Okay. What do I need to know?"

Fuck. Where did I even begin? "He needs to be in a relaxed environment as much as possible. No parties. No loud, sudden noises. He tries to push it. He thinks if he exposes himself to the shit that sets him off that it'll desensitize him to it, but that doesn't work. Video games with shooters can be a trigger. The smell of smoke. If he doesn't sleep for more than three days he's got pills he's supposed to take to help with that. They knock him out, but he wakes up feeling hungover so he doesn't like taking them, but if he's not sleeping he has to. It gets worse when he doesn't."

She nods. "Okay. I can look out for that."

I take a breath and tell her the last thing. "If you startle him, he can lash out. Physically. He pulls himself back once he recognizes you, but he's landed a punch a time or two. For me, that's not a problem. With you or another chick, it will be. Don't surprise him. If you walk in a room and he's spacing out, call his name. Don't touch him until he acknowledges you. And if he shifts, do not fucking run. He will give chase. Right now his tiger is fighting for dominance, so he needs to stay in his human skin as much as possible, but if he happens to shift and it isn't intentional, know that the beast is in the driver's seat. Don't provoke his instincts. Got it?"

"Yeah. I got it."

"Good. I'm gonna make a few calls and get that flight sorted out. Let me know if shit changes with him or if you need me for anything else."

She nods and I go to my room to make the call. My parents will kill me for this. Not because they give a shit if I use the jet, but because we had an agreement I wouldn't use Pierce assets unless I was willing to be an active member of the family—which I'm not—but it'll take them a while to notice, and what they don't know won't hurt them. It'll just bite me in the ass later.

# Chaper Nineteen
## Meiying

He isn't wearing a shirt. I don't know why I'm hung up on that, especially when I've seen him shirtless before a shift over a dozen times, but there he is, standing in the kitchen barefoot, wearing gray sweatpants without a shirt on.

I somehow manage to step farther into the room. He's at the stove, spatula in hand, and he's making … I peer around him … pancakes. Desmond is making pancakes. What twilight zone did I just walk out of? Shifters like meat on top of meat on top of more meat for breakfast, so the fact that he's making what I can only categorize as comfort food is … well … unsettling.

"You're up," he says without turning around.

I clear my throat. "Yeah."

"Have a seat. I'm almost done."

I nod, not that he sees it, and take a seat at the kitchen island, watching the muscles in his back flex as he moves around the kitchen, grabbing syrup and peanut butter before plating the pancakes and setting everything down in front of me. The pancakes are for me? And he somehow knows I like mine slathered with peanut butter before drenching them in syrup. How? And better yet, why?

"You hungry?"

I shake my head.

"When's the last time you ate?"

I think about it, but I don't really remember. "How long has it been since …" I can't say it, but he knows what I mean right away and curses softly under his breath.

"You need to eat. I brought food to your room. Why didn't you eat any of it?"

"I'm not hungry."

"I don't care." He tosses two pancakes onto a new plate, spreads peanut butter on both and then drizzles them with syrup before sliding it across the counter to me. "Eat."

I stare down at the food. My stomach twists into a knot and my eyes fill with moisture. I like pancakes like this because it's how Mom always made them for me.

"Dammit." He walks around the counter until he's right beside me. "You're wasting away. You need to eat something. Just a few bites, okay?"

I nod, forcing back the tears. I pick up the fork and knife and cut into the pancakes, finding tiny bits of bacon inside. If I wasn't on the verge of tears right now I would seriously appreciate this, because duh, bacon!

Desmond grabs his own plate and fills it with bacon, eggs, and a single piece of toast. But no pancakes. I frown down at my plate. "Why aren't you having any pancakes?"

"Not in the mood for any."

"Then why did you make pancakes if you knew you weren't going to eat any?"

He grunts. "You order pancakes every time we go to Sun Valley Station. Figured if I was going to get you to eat something, this was my best bet. You mentioned before that pancakes were your favorite food group."

"You remembered that?"

He nods.

I smile at that. Pancakes are my favorite food group. Mom used to make them on Sundays. Always with peanut butter and syrup, how her mom used to make them when she was growing up. The bacon is a new addition, and one I'm not upset over one bit.

A fresh wave of grief sweeps over me and I blink back the tears, eyes locked on my plate.

Desmond either doesn't notice or chooses not to mention it, which I'm grateful for. "I have practice today. I missed earlier this week, which was fine, but we have a game tomorrow and I have to show up. Will you—"

"I'll be fine."

He frowns. "That's not what I was going to ask."

Oh. "What were you going to ask?"

He looks at me, looks at my plate, then waits. I sigh and take a bite.

He grunts. "I was going to ask if you'd come to campus with me.

Zheng had to fly out to Florida to take care of a few things, and I don't like the idea of leaving you here alone."

"I—"

He cuts me off. "There's a lounge area just off the locker rooms where you can hang out. Maybe catch up on homework or watch some brainless T.V. on the television inside. We usually watch game tapes, but I think Coach has it hooked up to cable."

I worry my lower lip. "I'd rather stay here."

His muscles flex and he takes a bite of his food, chewing while he thinks. "Practice is less than two hours. I can leave early if I need to. You won't have to be there long."

I shake my head. "I don't want to go. I never should have gotten up. I'll just go back to the room and—"

"Meiying, I'm not leaving you here alone. Right now isn't the time for you to be difficult. Change your clothes if you want to, but you're coming."

I look down at myself. I'm still wearing his shirt. It's been several days. Almost a week and I'm still in the same shirt. The same pair of underwear. Oh god. I probably smell awful, and of course he can smell me. Hell, I can smell myself.

"If it's quick, you have time for a shower."

I swallow hard and nod. "Fine."

"Really?"

"Yeah. But I want a shower first."

He exhales a harsh breath. "Okay. Good. Eat some more first. We'll leave in an hour."

I take another bite, barely tasting it, but it seems to make him happy. My stomach growls, so I must be hungry. I just don't *feel* hungry. I'm numb. Empty.

I force myself to eat one whole pancake before pushing my plate aside. "I need to go back to my place. I don't have any clothes or—"

"Your uh, big sister, what's her name? The witch girl."

"Quinn."

"Right. She packed up some of your things. Clothes. Toiletries. They're in the bag on the bathroom counter. If you're missing anything we can stop by and grab whatever it is on the way."

Oh. That was nice. "Okay. I'll go see what I've got." I hesitate. "After practice, are you taking me home?"

Some emotion flashes in his eyes, too fast for me to catch before he shakes his head. "No. You're going to stay here." Something like relief settles in me, but that's strange. Why would I be relieved about staying here? I don't like Desmond. We were literally fighting just a few days ago.

"For how long?"

He shrugs and goes back to his plate. "Until I decide you're okay."

My mouth tightens, and I consider arguing before my shoulders sag and I turn away. "Fine." I head for the bathroom to shower. I'll fight with him another day.

Desmond parks the Escalade near the athletic building, and before I even unbuckle, he has my door open and is helping me out of the car.

Why is he being so nice? Nice and Desmond Pierce don't go together. I mean, I know my mom just... the word stalls in my brain and I take a moment to breathe through it. Whatever the reason, I don't want him to be nice to me. I need things to be normal. I don't want his or anyone else's pity.

I tug my hand out of his as soon as I'm out of the car. He grabs a gym bag from the back and then we're cutting across the parking lot to the main doors. Inside, I ignore the students in the halls and follow Desmond to the locker room. He opens the door and loud voices can be heard. Blocking my sight, he takes me down a row of lockers before stopping at a closed door. He pushes it open and checks inside before backing up and holding it open for me.

"Yo, Pierce!" someone calls.

"Give me a minute," he shouts back. To me he says, "You can hang out here. No one will bother you."

We step into a medium-sized room. There are a few sofas scattered around the room and a large flat screen T.V. mounted on one of the walls. "There's a bathroom through that door." He points to the left. "And I'll have Coach hang on to my phone. If you need anything, call me. I'll be done in an hour and a half. Two, tops."

I nod and take a seat on the nearest sofa.

"You're not going to wander off, right?"

"I'll be here."

He stares at me as if gauging my intent. "Good. If any of the guys come in here, tell them to get the fuck out. Got it?"

"Yep."

He closes the door behind him and I take a steadying breath. I find a remote between the cushions and flick on the T.V., stopping on a Disney movie. I don't have it in me to watch anything heavier than that. My phone rings. Zheng's name flashes across the screen. Shit. I haven't even talked to my brother yet. I should have. But I haven't.

I'm not sure what to say to him, and I'm almost certain he hasn't known what to say to me, but he's in Florida handling things I know I'm not in the right headspace to handle, so I need to answer.

I hit accept and bring the phone to my ear. "Hey."

He's quiet on the other end before I hear him release a breath. "Hey."

That one word, hearing his voice, has emotions clogging my throat. "You good?" I ask.

He forces a laugh. "I should be asking you that."

Yeah. Maybe. "I'm okay."

Another heavy breath. "That's good. Des's not being an asshole is he?"

A small laugh. "No. He's being nice, which is … weird. I kinda wish he'd be an asshole."

I curl my legs beneath me and sink into the sofa. "Are you calling because…" I swallow hard. "Did you need…" I don't know how to get the words out.

"Yeah. Sorry. I wanted to ask if you were okay with Mom being cremated. It's a lot easier to get her back if we do but if you don't want that—"

"It's fine," I choke on the words.

"Are you sure?"

"MmHmm." My heart squeezes in my chest. We weren't very

religious, but I know Mom is—was—Catholic. She'd have wanted a proper burial, but I don't think either Zheng or I can go through with one. This, this is better. "Maybe we can sprinkle her ashes in the ocean or something. Mom might have liked that."

"You think so?" His voice is thick.

I have to blink back my tears before I can answer. "Yeah. I think she would. Remember when we were kids and we went to Myrtle Bay? You got stung by a jellyfish and freaked out trying to pee on your own leg."

He groans, but manages a laugh too. "You promised never to bring it up again."

I snicker. "I know, but we should go there. We used to go every summer growing up. Mom loved that place."

"Yeah, she did, didn't she?"

I sit still, holding the phone tight as we both listen to the other breathe. "I miss her," I tell him, hating how my voice quivers.

"I miss her, too."

This is hard. My eyes fill with tears again, and no matter how hard I fight to hold them in, they still spill down my face. "Will you be home soon?" I ask, needing to say something to fill the silence.

He coughs, clears his throat. "Yeah. I'll be back in a few days. We can figure out what to do after that. There's no rush, okay? We can take however long we want."

I bob my head up and down. "Okay."

"I gotta go, but I'll try and check in later. You'll be okay with Desmond?"

I swallow past a lump. "Yeah. I'll be okay."

"I love you, sis."

"Love you, too." Zheng hangs up and I just sit there, unmoving. I don't know for how long or what time it is when all of a sudden the door opens and Deacon steps in the room.

I look up at him, tears still running down my face, and he drops down in front of me. "Hey, are you okay? Are you hurt?" He checks me over as I sit there, frozen in place.

"Meiying." He cups the sides of my face. "What's wrong? Why are you crying?"

I look down at my phone. It's still in my hand, fingers gripping it tightly. Deacon sees it and gently pries it from my fingers, setting it beside me. "You're kinda freaking me out here," he says. "I saw you come in with Desmond, figured I'd check in on you. I can't believe he left you in here like this."

I shake my head. "He didn't. I—" *Come on Meiying, pull it together.* "I'm sorry." I blink. "I was just talking to my brother. I..."

His gold-colored eyes stare into me, seeing more than he should. I want to curl into a ball and hide. Turn off the lights and just pretend today isn't here. "Come on." He pulls me to my feet.

"Where are we going?"

"You need chocolate. Or cake. Or both. We're going to get some of that."

I side-eye him as he steers me out of the room. "Why do I need chocolate? And don't you have practice?"

He shrugs, his hand on my lower back as he leads me outside. "I have sisters. When they cry, I give them chocolate. It's the one thing

I never get wrong and it works every time, so that's what we're going to do. Come one, there's a vending machine just down the hallway."

I nod but... "What about practice?"

"Desmond is running plays today, so it's fine. No one will miss me."

"Oh. Alright then." We find the vending machine and he shoves a few dollar bills in, getting a Reese's, Snickers, Hershey bar, Milky Way, and a Fast Break. Arms full, we find a few lounge chairs to sit in and he drops the candy in my lap.

When I don't move to open any, he grabs one of the bars—a Snickers—and peels the wrapper back before handing it to me. "Try it. I swear it works."

I give him a disbelieving look, but take a bite anyway, letting the chocolate melt on my tongue. I chew and swallow before taking another bite, and the next thing I know, the Snickers is gone and I'm moving onto the Peanut Butter Cups.

Three candy bars in and I feel more like myself. I've wiped the tears from my face, and Deacon catches me up on some of what I've missed in our English class. Twenty minutes goes by, and for the first time in nearly a week I feel like I can breathe. This distraction, it's exactly what I need.

I look down at the last candy bar in my lap and know I'll regret it later, but I peel back the wrapper and take a bite anyway. I moan. Fast Breaks are my favorite, so I saved the best for last.

"You cannot make sounds like that," Deacon says, a small smile on his face.

I roll my eyes. "You'd moan if you had this in your mouth."

He chokes, but covers it with a cough. "You can't say things like that to me either."

I grin. "Want a bite?" I ask him, but a commotion down the hallway catches my attention and I turn. "Shit," I whisper. Desmond is storming toward us, shirt drenched in sweat and a pissed-off expression on his face.

He's already yelling before he's even next to me. "What the hell were you thinking?" he shouts, coming to a stop beside us. "Do you have any idea how worried I was when I opened the door and you weren't there? *Fuck*." He turns around, hands on his waist and takes a few steps away before turning back to me. "You said you'd stay put. Why did you—" It's then that he notices Deacon. His eyes darken and I jump to my feet.

"Look, I'm sorry. I should have left a note or something."

He scoffs. "Right. A note would have helped."

My anger spikes. I'm not a child. I don't need to be coddled and looked after. "You know what? Fine. I'm not sorry." I turn to Deacon. "Thanks for the chocolate and for helping with," I wave to my face, "all of this. It was nice to feel like me for a little bit."

He stands. "Anytime you need a good laugh and some chocolate, give me a call. You don't have to tell me your personal shit, but if you wanna hang, I'm around."

"Thanks. I appreciate that."

He pulls me in for a hug, releasing me just as quickly when Desmond makes a sound in the back of his throat, low and threatening. "I'll catch you later, beautiful," Deacon calls over his shoulder, and then it's just Des and I.

I sigh and pick up the candy wrappers that fell when I stood up. I shove them in the trash bin and wait for Desmond to yell at me some more, but he doesn't. Instead, he has this pensive look on his face and he refuses to look at me. Somehow, it's worse than the yelling.

When we get outside he opens the door for me, closing it once I'm safe inside the Escalade. I put on my seat belt as he gets inside and I fiddle with the music knob as he pulls out of the parking lot. Five minutes into the drive and he still hasn't said anything.

I hate it.

"Look, I'm sorry. Okay? Can you stop giving me the silent treatment already?"

"I'm not giving you the silent treatment."

I huff. "Then why are you so silent?"

He glares at me. "Do you all of a sudden want to talk? You've barely said a word in five fucking days, but I leave you alone for an hour and suddenly you're chatting with Deacon. My bad. Figured I must be the one guy you refuse to talk to."

I lean my head against the window, the cool glass chilling my skin. "I'm not refusing to talk to you," I tell him.

He grunts. "But you'd rather talk to Deacon?"

"No. I..." I try to put my thoughts into words, but it all sounds so stupid. "Deacon isn't treating me differently."

Desmond scowls. "What the hell does that mean?"

"You're being nice. Like really nice. You check on me all the time. You made me pancakes. You open my door for me."

"So what, I'm supposed to be a dick even though your mom just died?"

My breath hitches and Desmond mutters a curse. "I didn't mean—"

"That," I yell at him. "That, right there. You keep doing things like that. You're apologizing to me when before, you never would have said 'I'm sorry.' That isn't you. That's not us. Not how we communicate."

"You're not making any sense."

"I don't want you to treat me any different. I need things to go back to how they were. The bickering. You being an insensitive jerk."

"I'm not insensitive."

"Yeah, you are. You kissed me when we were in high school and pretended like it never happened. You told me I was shallow. That I couldn't keep a guy's attention. And then gave me the best orgasm of my life, and after, pretended like it never happened. You humiliated me at the Kappa Eagle party, made me get out of the pool, basically said I looked like a slut and when I stripped naked in front of you, you left, and big surprise, you pretend it never happened. I'm sorry, how is none of that insensitive? Did you actually consider my feelings even once before doing any of those things?"

He's quiet.

"No. You didn't. And it's fine."

He bangs his head back on the headrest. "It's not fine."

"Yes, it is. It's fine because it's you. It's what I expect. You're a jerk to me. I'm a bitch to you. But this, whatever this version of you is that's nice to me, I can't deal with it right now. I need you to be the same guy you were a week ago. Don't coddle me. I'm not a piece of glass. I won't break."

We pull into his driveway and he turns off the car, neither of us getting out. "You want me to be a jerk."

"Yes."

"Fine. Your mom died almost a week ago, and you're being a baby. You've been hiding in your room for too fucking long and you're wasting away. You've lost weight. You look like shit. And your brother has enough on his plate that he has to deal with, but instead of handling what he needs to, he's calling me five times a day to check on you when he shouldn't have to. Pull yourself together, figure out what you need to do to grieve, and get on with it."

I suck in a shuddering breath and squeeze my hands into fists on my lap.

"Shit. I went too far."

I press my lips together, blinking back the tears and shaking my head. "I'm fine." I tell him, but it's a lie. There's this hole inside of me and his words, hearing about Zheng, it punches the hole wide open. I'm so fucking selfish. My brother shouldn't have to check in on me.

I fight to keep it together. I told Des to be mean. He did what I asked, so why does it hurt?

He opens his door and the next thing I know he's right beside me, reaching over my lap to unbuckle me. "I'm sorry. I didn't mean any of it. I thought ... I thought this is what you wanted. I thought it would help."

Like a dam breaking, my tears fall down my cheeks.

"Fuck."

I was falling apart. Again. I had an hour where I kept it together and now I was crumbling.

Des slides his arms beneath me and carries me out of the car. Cradled in his arms, he manages to get us inside and into the living room. My arms are wrapped around his neck, as though holding onto him will somehow hold me together.

He sits on the sofa, still cradling me in his arms. It's intimate and comforting and even knowing I'll hate myself for it tomorrow, I cling to him and cry into his chest.

I feel like pieces of me are breaking one by one, the pain growing more and more with each breath until it's too much. I want to scream, but nothing can get out past the tears. My shoulders shake and I wheeze, unable to catch my breath. Why does it hurt so fucking much?

"Meiying, please." He presses his lips to my temple. "You're killing me here, kitten. What can I do?"

# Chaper Twenty

## Meiying

"What can I do?" he asks again, and there is something close to panic in his voice. Emotion clogs my throat, threatening to suffocate me, and no matter how hard I try, I can't swallow it down. I try to draw on my tigress, but she's just as devastated as I am. Neither of us able to cope with the loss of my mother.

I try to speak. To tell him it hurts too much. I don't want to live like this. But I choke on my words, unable to get them out. I scream, choking on my tears as Desmond holds me in place, a wild look in his eyes. One hand grips the back of my neck, the other clutches my hip. "Meiying, I don't know how to fix this. How to fix you. What can I do?" He is almost begging and Desmond never begs, but ...

Nothing. There isn't anything he can give me that will make this go away. Nothing that will bring my mom back. I want to shift and run away and never come back. Lock away all of these human emotions and surrender to my pain.

"I don't want to … feel like… this. It hurts… too much," I finally manage to tell him.

He curses and a nerve jumps in his neck. "I can feel your struggle with your beast. You can't give in to her, kitten. You can't slip down that slope. You won't come back. Do you understand?"

I blink through my tears but only manage to shake my head. I hear the words he's saying. I know he's right. But I don't care. I want to slip into oblivion, and if that means I lose my humanity along with this pain, so be it.

I pull at my shirt, tugging it over my head in jagged movements.

"What are you doing?"

"I need to shift. I—"

He snarls and presses his face against mine, our foreheads nearly touching. "No," he snarls, his eyes glowing with the force of his wolf, and I can hear the command in his voice. It's an Alpha's command, and a small piece of me demands I submit to that command. That I obey him. But I'm so lost to my grief that it can't take hold and I quickly brush it aside.

I move to tug down my skirt but he grabs my jaw, forcing me to still. "You can't shift. Not when you're like this. You'll lose yourself—"

"I don't care!" I snarl in his face and pound my fists against his chest. "I don't—" a shuddering breath, "—want to feel like this. I can't, Des. Please."

"*Fuck*. Meiying, you have to work with me here. If you go rogue, I'll be forced to put you down. Don't put me in that position. You can't do that to me. Do you hear me?"

I shake my head. No. "Please."

He moves his hands to either side of my face, leaning in until we're only an inch apart and his warm breath caressing my skin.

"You can't go down that path. We'll find another way. Come up with something to help—"

"Like what? What could possibly help me? What will fix my mom being dead? Huh?" I wail.

He offers no answers.

Tears spill from my eyes and hopelessness slams into me. "I hate you," I tell him. "I hate you. I hate you. I hate you."

"I hate you, too," he tells me, but the way he says it doesn't sound like he's telling me he hates me at all. It sounds like he's saying something else entirely.

"I don't want to feel like this anymore." I don't want to feel at all.

"I know, kitten. I know. If I could make the pain go away, I would. Fuck, I'd do anything to make it go away right now. But I won't allow you to lose yourself to your beast. Anything but that, kitten."

There's that endearment again. I know it means nothing. He's just being nice to me. Using comforting words, but what if it's more than that? Or what if it can be more than that? At least for a little while.

I reach for him, shifting in his lap. "Help me?" I ask.

He holds me tight against his chest. "Anything, Meiying. Just tell me what to do. What will make it bearable right now? This very moment? What else can I do? I can't see you like this and not do something. I have to do something."

I don't let myself think about it. I lean back in his embrace and when he tilts his chin down to look at me, his eyes full of concern, I kiss him.

He responds immediately, his hold shifting until he's grasping the side of my neck and angling me for a deeper kiss. Hot. Desperate. I pour everything I'm feeling into that kiss. My hurt. The pain. The anger over it all.

Our teeth clash. Our tongues duel. He slides his fingers into my hair and devours my mouth. There is no other way to describe it, and the longer he kisses me, the further the pain fades into the background. It's still there, lurking in the shadows of my mind. I'm not naive enough to think kissing Desmond will make it go away forever, but it helps. It gives me something else to think about. Something else to feel.

But I need more.

I shift until I'm straddling his lap and rock myself against him.

He growls, a sound full of need before breaking the kiss. "Meiying..."

I see my own desire reflected back in his eyes. He wants this just as much as I do. We may not get along. Hell, we might even hate each other, but this, this he can do. This will help.

"Are you sure?"

My eyes narrow and I shift on his lap, grinding against the hard-on he's sporting beneath me. That should be his answer.

"Fuck."

He captures my mouth again. After that, it's a flurry of frenzied movements as we tear at one another's clothes. He doesn't bother to peel them off me and neither do I. Claws tip the fingers of both our hands as we partially shift and rip one another's clothes off, the scraps of fabric falling to the ground like tattered ribbons until I'm left standing naked before him.

Desmond cups my breast and I arch closer to his touch, throwing my head back as he squeezes me in his hand. His touch is rough. Bruising. And I relish it.

"We should move," he mumbles against my lips, but I don't let that deter me. I slide my hand beneath his briefs, wrapping my fingers around him and giving him a firm stroke.

"Jesus Christ," he snarls.

The next thing I know, he's on his feet, my legs wrapped around him. He carries me to his room, closes the door behind him, and then tosses me on his bed, my back sinking into the soft mattress. He doesn't miss a beat. In a flash, he's on me. His powerful body pressing firmly against mine.

He kisses me again and I gasp, his tongue seeking out my own and sliding into my mouth. I moan. He tastes so good. Like coffee and spice. His underwear rubs against my core, the thin barrier still separating us, and I immediately hate it. I don't want anything between us. I need to feel his skin on mine. Every damn inch of it.

I claw at his boxer briefs and he smacks my hand away and seizes control, removing the last of his clothes before he runs his thumb over my nipple and slides down my body to take one in his mouth.

I whimper.

He peppers kisses across my chest before swirling my other nipple with his tongue.

"Desmond, please."

He glances up at me, his eyes molten with his wolf. He watches my face as he kneads my breasts, cataloging every gasp and moan I make. He pinches and pulls on my nipples.

"You're so fucking responsive."

My breathing is heavy as he slips further down the bed until his broad shoulders are nestled between my thighs. He spreads my legs open, and as his face stares down at my sex, his warm breath fans across my skin. I could die and go to heaven with the way he is looking at me right now, his gaze hot and hungry. Like I'm his last meal and he can't wait to devour me.

He doesn't give me the chance to speak. To get nervous. He locks his hooded gaze with mine and presses a hungry kiss to my core, using his thumbs to spread me open even more.

"Shit," I gasp.

He chuckles, sliding his hands under my thighs and cupping my ass as he tilts my pelvis closer to his mouth. "You like that?"

My teeth sink into my bottom lip, and I nod.

"I can smell your need. It's intoxicating."

He leans in again and his mouth latches onto my pussy. I cry out, throwing my head back against the bed. He licks my slit before spearing his tongue inside me, and after only a few strokes, the pressure begins to build.

My pussy clenches and my legs quiver as he teases me, licking and sucking, but never putting enough pressure on my clit to throw me over the edge. I thrust my hips up to meet his touch, my body desperate for more friction.

I'm wound so tight I feel like I'm about to snap.

"Desmond!"

He grabs my hips with bruising force, pinning me to the bed, and begins to eat my pussy like a man starved. It only takes another minute until I'm crying out and bucking against him, but he doesn't let up. He locks onto my clit, my body hyper aware and overly sensitive as wave after wave of pleasure slams into me. I cry out again with the force of my release and Desmond growls, a hungry and distinctly wolfish sound that rumbles against my sensitive flesh, sending aftershocks through my system.

Limp and sated, my legs shamelessly drop to the bed. I struggle to catch my breath. My vision spots with black and my head spins.

I expect Desmond to stop. To climb back beside me, but he stays rooted between my legs. His mouth still between my thighs. When I feel like my heart is no longer at risk of beating out of my chest, he flicks his tongue over my sensitive clit.

I moan. My tigress watches him through my eyes, apprising him as someone worthy. Someone who demands her attention.

Desmond presses his palm over my stomach, holding me down as he devours me all over again, only this time he nudges one thick finger inside me.

My muscles tense, legs quivering. I growl as he strokes me. "Oh, god."

"Fuck, you're tight," he murmurs against me right as a second orgasm hits me out of nowhere and I grind against his hand, riding out my release.

Desmond leans back, his eyes taking me in. "Better?" he asks, rising to his feet with an arrogant smile on his lips..

I push myself up to my elbows. My hair sticks to my neck and forehead and I brush it back away from my face. "Desmond," I growl when he doesn't move closer. "Are you going to stand there or are you going to fuck me?"

His eyes darken, a savage expression passing over his face. "I don't think we—" He hesitates. "We don't need to do that. I can make you feel good in other ways."

Common sense dictates I listen. I haven't slept with anyone before, and a grief-induced fuck fest isn't how I imagined my first time, but I'm past the point of caring. I want this. Need it. And my beast agrees.

"If you don't want me—"

"I'm not saying that."

I swallow and can feel myself being pulled under again. A mess of emotions swirling inside me. No. No. NO!

I blink quickly as I bite out my words. "Then what are you saying?"

He rubs his jaw, my release still glistening on his lips. "You want me to fuck you?"

"Yes." I thought I made myself clear already. "I'm not going to force myself on you. If you don't want this, want me in this way, I can find someone else—" I say, though the very idea of someone else makes my lip curl. I don't want someone else. I want him.

"The hell you will," he snarls.

Desmond grips his cock, drawing my attention to his erection. I swallow hard and a thread of doubt worms its way inside of me. Will it fit?

Without breaking eye contact, he leans to the side and retrieves a condom from the nightstand. He tears the foil packet with his teeth and shamelessly rolls the condom onto his shaft before stroking himself again.

"Say it again," he grinds out as he climbs onto the bed, positioning his cock at my slick entrance. "Tell me what you need."

"I need you to fuck me."

He makes an animalistic sound in his chest, and the head of his cock slides between my folds but without entering me.

"If you regret this in the morning—"

"I won't," I assure him.

Blind desire flashes across his face, but rather than sinking into me as I expect, he sits back on his heels and flips me onto my stomach. My heartbeat kicks into overdrive as he pulls my hips toward him until I'm on hands and knees. My legs wide and my back arched for him.

"Des..." My voice quivers with need. In this position I'm vulnerable, and I don't know how to feel about that.

His cock rubs against me from behind.

I shift my hips back and turn my head to look at him. His face is locked in concentration, his expression predatory. "Spread your legs for me."

I do what he asks, widening my stance. He presses a hand against the center of my back. "Tilt your ass up," he orders, before sliding that same hand down between my legs. I try to tamp down on my nerves as Desmond presses a finger inside me, rubbing the walls of my pussy before he retreats and lines up his cock. Goosebumps break out across my skin and he leans forward, scraping his teeth over my bare shoulder as his hips thrust against me, his cock buried to the hilt in a single powerful move.

I cry out, a sharp stab of pain spearing into me.

He stills. "What the fuck?"

My legs tremble, but I manage to blindly reach back and grab hold of his wrist. "Don't."

"You're a virgin." He sounds both pissed off and in awe.

*Not anymore.* I think to myself, but don't say the words aloud.

"Why would you... why didn't... *fuck*."

My body is tight, my muscles clenching against the intrusion. I force myself to take a deep breath and relax.

Desmond leans over me, his forehead resting between my shoulder blades. "What were you thinking?" he whispers against my skin, the words almost reverent.

"Desmond?" I say through clenched teeth.

"Yeah?"

"Move."

He pulls back and for a second I think he's going to withdraw all the way and I panic. "Not stop," I clarify, and he stills. The head of his cock barely inside of me. "I need you to move."

He flexes his hips, an inch sinking back into my wet center.

I moan, tilting my hips in encouragement.

He curses.

"Your first time shouldn't be like this," he growls. "It should be with someone you trust. Someone—"

"Desmond." I give him a second. Looking back, I meet his conflicted gaze. "I trust you."

His nostrils flare and I can tell he's searching for the lie, but none exists. "You do?"

I nod. "Yes. Now please, fuck me already." He sinks in another inch, his eyes carefully watching me for my reaction. He's stretching me to my limits and I can scarcely breathe, but I don't want him to stop. It's the sweetest torture, and I need more of it.

He goes a little deeper.

My body is tight, my muscles clenching against the intrusion.

He pushes into me agonizingly slow until he's sheathed himself fully. He gives my body a second to adjust, and then he moves. In and out as he continues to thrust inside me. I grind my teeth together against the pain. It's not a lot, but enough to be uncomfortable. His body blankets me, his chin resting against my shoulder, breath against my ear. "Relax into it. Submit to me. Give me your body and let me make you feel good."

I fight against my instincts to deny him and do what he says, forcing myself to relax. The tension in my body melts away to be replaced with tingling sensations of need.

"That's it. Good girl."

He leans back, hands gripping my hips as he increases his pace.

I gasp when he hits a particularly sensitive spot. My mind goes blank and all I can think about, all I can feel, is Desmond moving inside of me.

I push back on my knees, meeting him thrust for thrust, and then

I'm coming again, my release spilling out of me on a guttural moan.

He slides out of me and flips me onto my back before sliding right back in, barely missing a beat. He hooks one arm under my knee, lifting my leg up and out to achieve a deeper angle.

I cling to his shoulders as he pounds into me, neither of us saying anything over the sounds of our flesh coming together. One of his hands cups the back of my neck and I stare into his eyes, even as I raise my hips to meet him.

His thrusts come faster, his face tight with tension as he surges inside me. "This what you need?" He forces out the words. I know what he's asking, so I don't hesitate to answer.

"Yes. More. Over and Over." I want to fall asleep from exhaustion. I don't want to lie here and think about my dead mom. About the pain or how helpless I feel. "Fuck me and don't stop. Okay? Not until I pass out. Until neither of us can go anymore."

A tremor moves through him and he nods. Good. We're in agreement.

His mouth crashes down on mine. His tongue licking against my own and his teeth scraping over my bottom lip. At some point the sun sets and the light coming through the windows dims. His forehead rests against my shoulder and my hands cling to his back, nails digging in when he stiffens and groans, pumping out his release.

He slumps against me, our breathing loud in the room. He takes a moment to catch his breath before sliding out of me. I hiss, but don't say anything. Desmond pulls off the condom, leaving to get rid of it before pulling another one out and setting it on the nightstand. I'm not sure how long a guy needs to recover, but he doesn't let me think about it long before he's reaching for me, his fingers sliding between my legs. First, he inserts one finger. Then a second. He works his fingers inside of me, rotating and rubbing every inch inside of me as he thrusts them in and out.

He adds a thirds and I cry out, his mouth crashing over mine and swallowing my cries.

I don't know how long he finger fucks me. Long enough for me to come again and for him to get hard. When he pulls out of me, he licks my juices from his fingers and slides the new condom over his cock.

He positions himself at my entrance again and I nod, letting him know I want this. Want more. He slides into me in a single thrust, a curse slipping past his lips.

"Yes," I tell him. "Don't stop."

We fuck two more times before we're both incapable of moving. After he disposes of the condom, I push up to leave. My legs feel like rubber and my head spins, but I think I can make it back to the guest room, only Desmond stops me.

He slips back into bed beside me and grabs me from behind, pulling my hips against his. My back to his front.

"Sleep," he grunts, tucking my head beneath his chin.

"But—"

"Sleep."

I take a deep breath, close my eyes, and for the first time in a long time, I do what Desmond tells me to do. I sleep.

# Chaper Twenty-One

## Desmond

I'm fucked. I am seriously and thoroughly fucked.

Harsh sunlight bleeds into the room. The clock on the wall reads eight AM. Late for me to be waking up, but not late enough that I need to hurry. Meiying is curled up in bed beside me, eyes closed, and jet black hair fanning around her pillow. I close my eyes for a beat, breathing in her scent. I stifle a groan. She smells *good*. The underlying scent of ginseng and oranges that is uniquely her wraps around me and urges my wolf to the forefront of my mind as if to claim her. As if I have that right.

I take in her delicate shoulders, the way she fits perfectly nestled in my arms, her ass pressing against my front. My dick stirs to life.

The thought of rolling her over and sliding my cock inside her wet heat has my dick jumping to attention and my wolf growing in approval. I press my hips against her and she lets out a breathy little sigh, not unlike a purr, and fuck does that turn me on as she presses deeper into me in her sleep. She feels good in my arms. Right. Like she belongs there. Which is why I can't stay in this bed any longer. If I do, I'm going to wake her up, fuck her, and then we'll both have to face the reality of what happened last night. I doubt she's ready for that. I know I'm not.

I slide my arm out from beneath her and climb out of bed, careful not to wake her. The sheet shifts with me, exposing her creamy skin and her perfect tits. Tits I had my hands on last night. My mouth on. I'm tempted to crawl back into bed, but it's a bad idea. This. Us. I shake my head. Her mom just died and what do I do? *Christ,* I'm a prick. I completely took advantage of her grief when … my mind wanders and I start to count the days. Shit. Shit. I cover my face with my hand. She's seventeen. *You took the girl's virginity at seventeen.* I rub the back of my neck. I didn't expect that. Most shifters begin sharing skin privileges much younger in our youth. We're tactile creatures, and our animals encourage us into physical relationships. We want the contact and affection that comes from being with someone. It soothes the animal inside of us. Gives them a necessary release and allows us to better maintain control.

That she waited this long, it means skin privileges are important to her. She doesn't give just anyone the right to touch her, and that she allowed me to be the one … I hang my head. It makes the possessive beast inside me lunge forward deep inside my chest demanding that we make her ours. Not just today but tomorrow and forever after that. Which is all sorts of fucked up.

Even I know how seriously screwed up last night was. All the lines I crossed.

Leaving her in my bed, I opt for a cold shower. But, five minutes in and my dick is still rock hard, like it knows Meiying is on the other side of the wall, naked and waiting. My wolf is riding me hard, and the urge to stalk back into the room and devour her like prey is damn near all consuming.

I fist my cock in my hand, stroking myself to relieve the pressure. I groan as flashes of her assault me behind my closed eyes. Her hair tangled in my hands. Her eyes alight with her beast. Her sinful mouth as I drive myself into her.

*Shit. I'm going to come.*

The shower curtain is pulled back and a very awake and very naked Meiying stands before me. She sees me, sees my fingers wrapped around my cock, and steps inside the shower, dropping to her knees to replace my hand with her own.

My dick jerks at her touch and a smile curls her lips.

*"Fuck."* What is this girl doing to me? "Meiying?" I growl. I'm not sure if it's a warning or a plea.

Her big blue eyes look up at me through her lashes, her fingers barely able to close around my length. My gaze drops to her mouth, and the image of her lips wrapping around the head of my cock has me straining painfully in her grip. It would be so easy to slip between her lips, and I know it'd feel good. A thought trickles into my mind, wondering if she's done this with another guy. Last night, I was the first to take her pussy. Would I be the first to take her mouth, too?

I want that. It's selfish and wrong, but I want all of her firsts.

Everything that she'll give me.

Her tongue darts out, licking the drop of pre-cum from my slit and I thrust forward, unable to stop myself. She smiles, and it undoes something inside of me.

"You can't touch me like that, kitten." My voice is hoarse, the tendons in my neck straining. "If you open that mouth of yours again. I'm going to take it." It's both a warning and a promise.

I'm clearly insane, or just a glutton for punishment and high on lust, because instead of pulling away from her touch, I press forward, rubbing my dick over her mouth, enjoying the sight of my lingering arousal as it paints her lips, making them glisten.

I put one hand against the wall to steady myself, the other fists the back of her head, holding her in place, but I don't push myself inside her mouth. She has to be the one to make that decision. She's gotta show me what she wants. What she's willing to give me. Because with how I'm feeling right now, I'll take all of it. Every piece of her she'll let me have.

"Have you sucked a man's cock before?" Her eyes are dilated, filled with lust and need as she bobs her head in confirmation.

I snarl, the wolf in me rising in fury that someone else would dare to touch what is ours. *Fuck.* I hate that answer. My grip in her hair tightens and she hisses, but she doesn't pull away. Good. I don't know what would happen if she did. The need to dominate her rides me hard, my chest heaving with harsh breaths as I fight to keep myself in check.

"You want my cock?"

Another nod.

Fuck it. I'm going to hell for this, but I was probably heading that direction anyway.

"Open your mouth, kitten. Suck my cock."

She widens her stance, a telling sign that she knows what's coming and she's accepting it. Bracing herself, but not to suck on my dick. She's bracing for me to fuck her mouth. And that's exactly what I intend to do.

Her lips part and like the impatient bastard I am, I thrust forward, filling her mouth until I reach the back of her throat. She doesn't gag or pull away like I expect her to. Instead, she relaxes her throat, opening her mouth wider, and takes more of me in. *Jesus Christ!*

Her eyes hold mine, tears leaking from the corners, but she doesn't let up. Her cheeks hollow out, sucking me harder while I pump my dick into her mouth.

"Fuck, yeah. Just like that," I throw my head back, groaning.

With both hands now, I hold the back of her head, pumping into her mouth, but it isn't enough.

A growl tears out of my throat, low and rough, my entire body tensing, but I don't want to come in her mouth right now. I want inside her cunt. I want her pussy milking my release from me as I bury my teeth in her shoulder and force her to submit to my beast, so that's what I'm going to have.

I grip her arms and jerk her to her feet. Wide eyes meet mine, but I don't answer the unspoken question in them. Turning off the water, I don't bother to dry off before I lift her out and set her down in front of the sink. I capture her mouth, my teeth tugging at her bottom lip.

"Are you wet for me, kitten?"

She moans into the kiss, her body shuddering in my arms. I slip two fingers into her, pushing in deep. She gasps against my mouth, her hands gripping my shoulders for support.

"So fucking wet," I murmur against her lips. I pull out, and instead of licking her juices from my fingers like I'm craving to do, I bring them to her mouth, pressing them between her lips. I'm transfixed, watching her mouth open, seeing her eyes shutter as she tastes herself. A small moan slips past her lips and my control shatters. I need her. Now.

I turn her away from me to face the mirror, her eyes holding mine with challenge as if telling me to do my worst. Her fingers splay on the counter and I step up behind her, a firm hand on her hip, the other between her legs. Her eyes hold mine captive as I scrape my teeth over her shoulder, and I see the moment she gives herself to me as her entire body shudders in anticipation.

I line my cock up with her entrance, her wet pussy coating my head, when I realize I'm bare. Shit. I suck in a breath and hold myself immobile. Meiying presses herself back and I grind my teeth together, my hand on her hip the only thing keeping her in place and preventing me from impaling her with my cock.

"I need to grab a condom," I bite out.

Her eyes widen with understanding, but neither of us move. Shit. Her juices drip over the head of my dick and goddamnit do I need to fuck her. The very idea walking away from her right now sends a physical stab of pain shooting straight through my cock.

"I'm on the pill," she says, voice soft. Hesitant. "I've been on it since

I was sixteen. I'm good."

Thank fuck.

I nod. "I'm clean," I tell her. Not that it's really a concern for our kind. It just seemed like the right thing to say.

Shifters can't contract STDs let alone any other virus or disease. The lycanthropy virus in our systems eradicates it should we ever become infected. I've never even heard of a shifter contracting a common cold. It just doesn't happen for us.

"Okay."

Okay.

I press into her, watching her face for a reaction as my cock slips between her folds. She gasps, head falling back on her shoulders to expose her neck in what I'm sure is a subconscious submission, because the Meiying I know would never bare her throat to me in offering.

Without even thinking, one hand slides up her body, stopping briefly to toy with one nipple, squeeze her full breasts, before wrapping around her throat in a possessive hold.

She moans, then hisses, as I thrust into her harder. Faster. "God, you're tight." I bite out the words as my hips pound furiously into her. I should slow down, ease her into this. She's got to be sore after last night, despite the Lyc-V in her system healing any injuries, but I can't muster the control needed to pull back.

She presses her ass into me, meeting me thrust for thrust. My hand flexes on her throat, her cries getting louder. "Oh, god," she moans, the walls of her pussy damn near strangling my cock. Her orgasm rocks through her, the scent of her need permeating the air and drawing my wolf forward. She arches her back, legs shaking, and I circle her clit, drawing out her release, demanding everything she has to give.

When her legs buckle, I push her forward, pinning her legs between me and the counter. With a hand on her back I push her down until her cheek is pressed against the mirror, her heavy breathing fogging up the glass and her tigress's eyes are reflected back to me through her gaze in the mirror.

My pelvis slams against her ass, my cock nudging her cervix as I bury myself deep. She isn't even trying to hold in her needy moans, which only serve to spur me on more. Her inner muscles clench around my dick, and I drive into her hard and fast, chasing my own release and grinding against her. Right as my balls draw up tight, muscles clenching, I lean forward and sink my teeth into her shoulder, pinning her down in the most primal way I can and with one final thrust and an agonizing groan, I spill my cum inside her.

My legs shake and I pull out, leaning back to stare at the mark I left on her. Already it's healing, and I hate that there will be no lingering reminder of what we did. That I can't mark her body as mine for others to see.

Meiying is still slumped on the counter. I turn the shower back on, checking the temperature to make sure it's ready before pulling her under the warm spray and washing the signs of sex from both our bodies. Neither of us speaks, but when I move to wash between her thighs, she slaps my hand away.

Right.

We don't do gentle or sweet. We fuck. She doesn't want tenderness from me.

Grabbing us each a towel we dry off and I get dressed by myself in my room. Meiying retreats to the guestroom where her clothes are and comes back a few minutes later wearing a pair of white cut-off shorts and a red top. She has a frown on her face and a determined look in her eyes.

"I have a game today," I tell her.

She nods. "You mentioned that yesterday."

"Do you want to come? Jo will be there. You won't be alone."

She bites her bottom lip, and I have to keep myself from going to her, tugging her abused lip free only to capture it with my own teeth to remind her that her mouth is only mine to abuse.

She doesn't answer.

"What's going on in that head of yours?" I ask, shoving my gear in my gym bag. Between sleeping in, the shower, and the sex, I'm running late and Coach will have my ass if I don't get a move on, but something is going on in that pretty little head of hers. I need to figure it out.

"Zheng will be pissed if he finds out about this."

I grunt. "I'm aware." I love the guy like a brother, and he loves me the same, but no way would he approve of what we've done.

"I don't want to be the reason you two have a falling out again. He needs you and the others too much."

I side eye her. "Spell it out for me, Meiying."

"You can't tell him. He can't find out about any of this." She indicates the space between us. I don't like the idea of being her dirty little secret. Not one fucking bit. But, I can't argue with her reasoning.

Liu has a lot on his plate. Me fucking his sister isn't something he needs to worry about right now. Not when me fucking his sister should never have happened in the first place. But after this morning, I can't say it won't happen again.

# Chaper Twenty-Two

## Meiying

I don't know what came over me this morning. But when I woke up and Desmond was gone, his scent still clinging to the sheets, a part of me crumbled, thinking he'd left me there, alone. Then I heard the water running and I just, I needed to know this wasn't going to be like all the times before. That he wasn't going to mess around with me, only to pretend nothing ever happened.

So, I went for broke, and for once in my life, I took my shot. I pulled back the curtain, standing naked and unashamed, and when I saw him standing there with his fingers wrapped around his cock, my need reflected in his eyes shining bright with his wolf, I wanted it to be my hand holding him. I wanted it to be my mouth bringing him his release.

He didn't push me away when I reached for him. He didn't tell me to stop or that he didn't want it. Want me. He moaned when I took him in my mouth. He growled and cursed when his dick bumped the back of my throat. And his body shuddered when he spilled his release inside me from behind.

This can't go anywhere. I know that deep within my bones. But I don't want to stop. I need whatever this is right now to chase away my grief. To push back the pain. I'm not stupid. I know who he is. Who I am. I'm not going to pretend that what we have is sunshine and butterflies with a happily ever after at the end of the rainbow. Because the fallout, if things take a bad turn, it isn't just the two of us who will be affected. I'm not sure what is going on with my brother, but I know it has to do with more than Mom. I can't be the reason he loses his best friend, and that's what will happen if he finds out. His protective brother streak won't allow it to be any other way.

"So we're on the same page, then?" I ask, needing confirmation.

Desmond releases a harsh breath and rubs his hand over the back of his neck. A muscle tics in his jaw, but after a few more seconds, he relents. "Fine, we'll be careful. Liu will never know I'm boning his baby sister."

I bark out a laugh. Way to be presumptuous. "You think this will happen again?"

He gives me a knowing look, his hooded gaze boring into mine. "You saying it won't?"

I manage a shrug. "Whatever we're doing here, it's casual."

"Agreed."

"This is not a relationship. We're not going to hold hands and go on dates."

He grunts.

"And no catching feelings," I tell him, as much for my own benefit as his. I silently remind my tiger that too, because she's already heading in the wrong direction.

"I wasn't planning on it."

"Good." I nod. "Zheng can't ever know—" He opens his mouth to interrupt but I rush on to finish, "I know. You said we'll be discreet, but I mean it. My brother can't find out about this. Not even years from now, okay? It never happened."

"Fine. Anything else?"

Nothing else comes to mind, so I shake my head.

"Okay. I have questions. I like shit to be black and white. No gray area." He sucks on his teeth, his expression letting me know he's not playing around.

"Alright. What are they?"

"You and Deacon, what's going on there?"

I shrug. "Nothing. He's nice to me. I told him at the start I was only interested in being friends. He's cool with it." Desmond scoffs, but I don't let it get to me. "Why? Because, just so we're clear, screwing my brains out doesn't mean you own me. You don't get to dictate who I talk to or who I'm friends with."

His jaw clenches and he grunts.

"Anything else you wanna know?"

"I know you think I get around"—I snort at that—"but if I'm fucking a girl more than once, she's the only girl I'm fucking, you feel me?"

I narrow my eyes, my tiger taking a sudden interest in our conversation. "What are you saying, exactly?"

"If you decide being *frien♦s,*" he growls, "with Deacon or anyone else isn't enough for you. If you want his dick or someone else's, do me a solid and let me know before you go testing the waters, alright? I'll be sure to give you the same consideration if I find myself in a similar situation."

Anger flashes through me at the thought of him with anyone else, and a snarl curls the edges of my mouth. He sees it, and a slow smile spreads across his face.

"Deal?" he asks.

I want to wipe the smug look off his face, but manage to grit out, "Deal."

"Last question." He waits until I nod. "Do you want a relationship? Is that what you're really looking for here?" His tone is even. His eyes not meeting mine. There is zero inflection in his voice to let me know if he's asking because he wants that, or if he hates the idea and just wants to make sure I don't want one too. My nostrils flare, but his scent gives nothing away. He's locked down his emotions, and I'm not entirely sure how to proceed.

I go with the response I think he's most after because right now, I need him to fuck me when I feel like I'm going to spiral and I need him not to be cagey about it. "With you? Definitely not." His eyes snap to mine, searching. "Look," I tuck my hair behind my ears and lay everything out for him. "You're arrogant, and most of the time, I can barely stand to be in the same room as you."

"The feeling is mutual."

"Right. So, a relationship would never work between us, assuming either of us even wanted one, but fooling around I'm fine with. Does that work for you? I don't need you to beat around the bush, either. I'm not a kid whose feelings you're going to hurt with a rejection." The silence stretches between us. "It's a yes or no question," I tell him, my patience growing thin.

He releases a breath, and without answering, he pulls me into his chest and slams his mouth down on mine. His kiss is all-consuming, leaving my head spinning and my heart racing out of my chest as he tastes my mouth, nips at my lips with his teeth.

A needy moan slips past my lips when he finally pulls away. Dark brown eyes meet my own, and in them I see my own desire reflected back to me. "This works for me," he says. Then he hesitates and asks, "When is your birthday? I know it's coming up, but I don't know the date."

"It was yesterday."

He pulls back, eyes wide. "You turned eighteen yesterday?" I nod. "And no one said shit? No one remembered, not even your brother?"

I shrug. "Shit happened. It's bad timing," I give him a considering look. "Or good, depending on how you look at it."

He smirks. "Yeah, I see what you're saying." He grabs his gym bag and heads for the door, pausing at the threshold to give me a backward glance. "Game's at eleven. I have to get to the field early and warm up." I nod, my lips pressing together. "Show up. I don't want you sitting there alone. You can call one of the girls for a ride if you don't want to drive yourself."

"I'll think about it," I say, and his eyes darken.

"I'll see you there. Eleven. And if you wear my number, I'll think about giving you a belated birthday gift." He gives me a heated look, and before I can respond, he's gone.

What the hell did I just get myself into?

We're just getting started with Desmond and Meiying.
Their story continues in
Cruel Promises and Twisted Temptations, coming soon.
If you're new to the series be sure to read
Wicked Wolves and Tangled Truths,
book 1 in the Blood & Magic: Hellbound series

**Dear Reader,**

**Thank you** for giving Cruel Wolves and Devious Deceptions a read. I know I left you a little bit hanging there but I promise it will all be worth it in the end.

If you're caught up on my Hellbound series and need something to binge while you wait for Cruel Promises & Twisted Temptations, check out my Blood & Magic Fireborn series which is complete at six books and begins with Cursed by Fire.

It's a slower burn romance with a lot of snark, action, and ass kicking.

Until next time...

xo Danielle


**P.S.** Reviews are like giving a hug to your favorite author. We love hugs. Please consider taking the time to leave a review for Cruel Wolves & Devious Deceptions on Amazon!

# More by Danielle Annett

## Blood & Magic: Fireborn
*SERIES COMPLETE*

Cursed by Fire

Kissed by Fire

Burned by Fire

Branded by Fire

Consumed by Fire

Forged by Fire

## Blood & Magic: Hellbound

Wicked Wolves & Tangled Truths

Savage Wolves & Dangerous Deals

Cruel Wolves & Devious Deceptions

Cruel Promises & Twisted Temptations

Angry Wolves & Sinister Secrets